BABY

DOCTOR

By Beau Brown

Prologue

Why was it doctor offices always had you sit in the main waiting room forever, and then when they finally called your name, you were just stuck waiting in another cramped room all over again? Did they think we didn't notice they were shifting us around like cattle? Why not just leave us in the main waiting room to begin with? Those were the sort of grumbly thoughts rolling around in my head as I checked my watch for the millionth time.

I shifted on the examination table, careful not to rip the paper that covered it. I rubbed my belly as I stared at the posters on the wall that showed diagrams of the omega pouch and the omega birth canal. I wanted a baby so bad. I'd dreamed of little else since I was young. But doctor visit after doctor visit always brought me the same depressing news; I wasn't able to get pregnant.

I sighed and scowled at the door. I'd been waiting so long I was fuming with irritation. I had a job. I couldn't spend my entire day here. I'd already waited three hours to see Dr. Hexton. The only reason I hadn't already stormed out was because he was the premiere fertility specialist in Poppy Field. I desperately wanted his expert opinion. If Dr. Hexton told me I couldn't get pregnant, then I couldn't get pregnant.

Please, please, please don't let him say that.

By the time the door finally opened, I was sweaty, annoyed and about ready to leave. Dr. Hexton walked in leisurely, as if he had no concept of time. He glanced up with a polite smile, and even as pissed off as I was with how long he'd kept me waiting, my stomach fluttered in response to his smile because he was gorgeous. I'd expected a much older man, but he was probably, at most, in his forties. His hair was dark with just a sprinkling of silver at the temples and his eyes were an intriguing golden brown.

"Good afternoon, Mr. Johnson." He gave me another courteous smile. "Have we seen you before?"

"No. This is my first visit here." I'd had to save up to see him. My health insurance would only pay for me to see the specialists in their medical group. But I'd wanted the opinion of the best in the field, and that had meant shelling out the dough myself in order to meet with Dr. Hexton.

"I see." He pulled on latex gloves as he said, "Would you mind lying down on the table for me? This won't take a minute."

I widened my eyes. "Oh, I thought I was just here for the blood test results."

He hesitated. "I don't believe in giving out a prognosis without physically examining my patients." His smile was a little more genuine. "Didn't you wonder why the nurse had you change into a gown?"

I laughed. "I was so nervous it didn't occur to me."

"I don't make people wear those silly gowns if I'm just giving them test results."

"That makes perfect sense. Like I said; I was distracted by my nerves." I lowered myself onto the table, sighing. My muscles were tense as he moved closer. I wasn't mentally prepared to be examined, so even though I tried to relax, it wasn't easy.

He lubed his gloved fingers and moved closer, reaching a hand under the paper gown. He avoided eye contact with me, instead staring at the center of my forehead. "I apologize. The gel will be cold at first."

"It's fine," I squeaked, grimacing as I sucked in a steadying breath. At the first touch of his fingers, I jumped, and he frowned. "Sorry," I muttered.

"Please try and hold still." His voice was gruff as his fingers gently probed the outside of my anus.

"Most guys buy me a drink before they get this far." I gave a weak smile.

A line appeared between his dark brows. "This is just a routine exam. I do hundreds of these a month. Just think of something pleasant and loosen your muscles." He sounded a little breathless, and he still kept his eyes pinned on my forehead.

"Okay. I'll try." His cologne was nice; citrusy and fragrant. He leaned his body against my side, and his fingers stroked the tender flesh around my anus as he sought my hole. I was embarrassed when the base of my cock tingled with arousal because of his touch. His seeking fingers were gentle, and the heat of his stomach against my hip had my cock twitching with interest. I was mortified and praying he didn't notice that my balls felt full and swollen as his wrist brushed them. When he slowly inserted a finger into me, it took all my self-control not to whimper with pleasure. I bit my lip, holding back the instinctive desire to press against his hand.

Fuck that feels good.

"That's right, now just relax." His voice was gentle, and he seemed unaware of my embarrassing arousal. "Just a little bit longer. Bear with me."

The slide of his finger inside me felt so delicious, I clamped my teeth. It had been far too long since anyone had touched me down there. I couldn't help but think about what a good lover the dear doctor probably was. If he could get me this turned on during an exam, just imagine the heights of pleasure he'd give if he was actually having sex with me.

Think about taxes or something. Think about anything but how nice his finger feels.

Trying to distract myself didn't work. My humiliation intensified as my breathing picked up, my nipples pricked and my cock hardened as his finger penetrated me further. Deeper and deeper, he slipped his fingers into my quivering body. My cock pressed the paper gown, and I opened my thighs wider; needing more.

Oh, fuck yes. Right fucking there.

"I'm sorry," he said softly. "I know this is uncomfortable for you."

"It's okay," I whispered, trying not to show how good his touch felt. Sweat broke out on my upper lip, and I tried to rein in my ridiculous arousal. He'd probably have been horrified if he knew the dirty thoughts rolling around in my head.

He's a doctor. He's not prepping me for intercourse.

I'd had at least twenty exams just like this one. Well, not quite like this one because he was the only sexy alpha fertility doctor who'd ever slid his fingers into my ass. But after all the times doctors had examined me, this was the only time I could remember it feeling delicious and sensual. Usually it was all very clinical and almost painful. But Dr. Hexton didn't just stick his fingers in and poke around like a plumber under the sink. He slowly caressed and explored my ass, and when his eyes dropped to mine, there was a strange moment where I knew he saw, and connected with me, as an omega, and not just as his patient. He quickly looked away, blinking rapidly as he pulled his fingers from my body.

"Okay. I think I have all the information I need to make an educated assessment." His voice was stiffer now, and he turned his back on me as he pulled off the gloves and tossed them into the trash.

I sat up, pulling the gown closed and trying to hide my erection with my arms. I breathed deep, attempting to squash my need for him to keep touching me. I cleared my throat. "I've... I've gone to every doctor in town."

"Is that right?" His voice was tight, and he still had his back to me.

"Yes. They always say the same thing; I can't get pregnant because my omega pouch is too small."

He snorted a sound of disgust. "Is that what they told you?"

"Yes."

He turned toward me, his eyes bright. "Hacks. They don't know what they're talking about."

I forgot all about my throbbing erection at his irritable statement, and a small glimmer of hope took root. "Really? You mean... you mean they were wrong?"

"Your omega pouch is of optimum size." His cheeks seemed pink as he continued, "In fact everything in that... region... seems to be of exceptional... quality. Your rectum is tight and supple." He cleared his throat. "Your ball sac is perfect, and of course your cock is a good length and width."

I laughed at his awkward compliment. "Thank you?"

He shrugged. "You'd be surprised how many omegas come to me worried about all of that."

"Oh."

"Omegas are always concerned with whether or not their alpha will find them adequate. I guess it's just in an omega's DNA to want to please their alpha."

"Yes. I guess." I lifted one shoulder. "I don't have that problem."

He raised one brow. "You shouldn't. You should have a very happy alpha."

I grimaced. "I mean I don't have an alpha."

He widened his eyes, looking surprised. "No?" He frowned. "You don't have an alpha?"

"No. He ran off with an omega who pops babies out like a rat. Just baby after baby," I grumbled. "I've struggled with my fertility."

"Oh, well, yes. Obviously. But babies aren't everything. You can still attract an alpha I'm sure. You're attractive and young." He grimaced. "Anyway—I digress."

My pulse skittered at his compliment. "No. It's nice to hear I'm probably not destined to a life alone. I truly thought I was screwed if I couldn't have kids. After talking to so many doctors and all of them saying my omega pouch was abnormal, I thought I would probably be alone forever." I sighed. "God, it's amazing to hear that you don't agree with them. That's such great news that my pouch is normal after all."

"Yes. I'm sure it is." He nodded, and he grabbed my chart again. "Your blood work is normal too."

"Most of the doctors said my blood was fine, but then they always got hung up on the size of my omega pouch." I laughed. "What a relief to know I can have kids after all." I slid off the table and pulled my underwear on. "I knew coming here was the right choice. Best hundred dollars I've ever spent."

He pulled his dark brows together. "Oh, I'm sorry. You must have misunderstood me."

I glanced up. "I'm sorry?"

He grimaced. "Mr. Johnson, I never said you could have children. Quite the opposite in fact."

Shock rattled through me. "What?" I whispered, feeling light headed. "But you just said my womb is the right size."

"It is."

"Then I don't understand."

"Your womb isn't the problem. You have issues that would prevent you from ever even conceiving." He bit his bottom lip when I gasped in horror. "It's just one of those things." His voice was matter fact.

"But... but..." I watched him, feeling as if my world had ended.

He sighed, seeming almost irritated that he had to explain further. "You see... when the omega pouch forms, its slightly raised to make room for the formation of the omega birth canal."

He folded his hands together as if showing me how it all worked. "It's really quite a remarkable design."

"I don't understand," I muttered, still reeling from his offhand announcement that I'd never have babies.

"In your case, the omega pouch is blocking your male ovaries. It's situated lower than usual."

"But... but you said it was fine."

"I said the size was normal. The placement is too low."

I could feel the blood draining from my face. "I've never heard of that," I whispered.

He gave me a sympathetic look. "I know. It's extremely rare. But with the pouch covering your ovaries, the odds of you ever conceiving are a bazillion to one. And I'm not using the term bazillion flippantly. You have far more chance of being struck by a meteor."

I stared at him with my eyes wide, and my stomach churning. "That's a horrible thing to say."

"Oh, I'm sorry. Really?" He frowned. "Well, regardless, it's the truth."

"But... you can't say things like that to someone. I have more chance of being struck by a meteor? That's awful."

"I don't see the point of beating around the bush."

"You just sound so heartless. You could try to at least *pretend* you care that you're giving me horrible news."

He rolled his eyes. "You omegas are so sensitive. You can't have babies. So what?"

My mouth fell open. "So what?" I leaned toward him, my face hot and my heart crushed. "My sole reason for existing is to have babies. What the hell good is an omega who can't have children? No alpha will want me. This is a life altering nightmare for me, and you sound like you told me you don't have my size loafers or something. I've wanted a baby for so long."

He squinted at me. "There are lots of other reasons to live. I mean, you can adopt a baby."

"I know, and that's definitely an option. But I've always wanted to experience carrying a child. I don't get to have that now, and you announced it to me as if it's nothing."

"I'm just trying to say you can still live a full life. Find an alpha who doesn't care about having babies."

"You and I both know that's no easy task."

"There are sterile alphas." He shrugged. "Perhaps you can find one of those."

I rubbed my face roughly, trying to control the depression that attempted to sink into my soul. "My life is over."

"Oh, come on now. I still say there are plenty of alphas who simply don't want children." He laughed stiffly. "I don't want kids."

I looked at him like he was crazy. "But you're the premiere fertility doctor in Poppy Field. How can you not want to have children?"

He shuddered. "I help *other* people have them. I don't want any. Not now, anyway. Goodness, the little brats drive me absolutely bonkers. They're noisy and selfish and they cost a fortune to take care of. No thank you."

"You're telling me you have no interest in carrying on the Hexton name?"

He curled his lip. "Not really." He sniffed. "My mother of course wants that. And I suppose eventually I'll have to settle down with an omega, and pop one kid out just to carry on the Hexton name. But I'm not looking forward to that, and that is a very, very, very long way off."

I shook my head in disgust. "I think I've heard about all I can take. If you don't mind, I need to get dressed so I can go back to work."

He cocked his head, looking puzzled. "Are you mad at me?"

I narrowed my eyes. "I'm not happy with you."

He chuffed. "But it's not my fault you can't have babies."

"No. I know. But it is your fault you're an insensitive clod."

"Excuse me?" He frowned.

"I can tell you don't know that you're coming off like a jerk, but you are. If you're going to work in this field, you need to sharpen your empathy skills. When you tell an omega they're barren—" My voice broke, and I wiped angrily at my teary eyes. "You're telling them the worst news possible other than death."

"But there are so many other things to live for," he said quietly, studying me closely. "I promise you that. Don't feel sad. You'll still have a happy life."

"You don't know that. You can't promise me that."

His expression was hard to read.

I lifted my chin, a painful lump in my throat. "Like I said, I have to get back to work."

He nodded and moved to the door. His dark eyes scanned me, and he looked unsettled. "You'll... you'll find an alpha, Peter."

His use of my name and heartfelt declaration was surprising after how cold he'd seemed earlier. But I was too upset about the news he'd given me to respond to him. I simply shrugged and turned my back on him to dress.

Chapter One

(One Week Later)

"You're depressed. Why would you go out to a club tonight?" Polly shook her head.

"Because what should I do? Sit around all night wondering who Carlos is fucking? I'm not doing that. I need to have some fun. I need to let loose tonight. You know... within reason." I frowned and poured more cream into my coffee.

"Honey, when you're like this, I know there's no talking to you. But you should be careful. The last thing you need is to get drunk and lose your wallet or something. You can barely afford to feed your parakeet."

I laughed. "I know. Don't worry. I won't do anything stupid. I wish you'd come with me. When was the last time you and I went out and just had some fun?"

She shrugged. "I have to work at four tomorrow morning. No way can I go out and party, then get up and work. Those days are long gone, baby."

I sighed. "I miss college. I liked being wild and irresponsible."

She grinned. "I know. God, those were the days."

I sipped my java, feeling depressed. I wasn't anything like when I'd been in college. I felt more hopeless these days. Maybe it was because I'd lost my alpha and found out I was barren all within the last month. I'd wanted babies so bad, and now that hope had been dashed.

Polly stood. "Well, have fun tonight. What are you wearing?"

"I don't know. But whatever it is, it will be tight and sexy."

She leaned toward me and waggled her finger in my face. "Don't forget to be careful."

I grimaced. "We both know I can't get pregnant. Hell, Carlos and I tried everything."

"And you're sure he wasn't shooting blanks?"

"If he was, that new omega he's hooked up with wouldn't be pregnant... again."

"I can't believe he got that omega pregnant while he was still with you." She scowled.

"Don't remind me. I can't believe he hid it from me so well."

"You're trusting. Most omegas are." She sighed.

My mouth drooped. "But I really, really, really wanted a baby."

"I know." She shuddered. "But better you than me, dear friend. I can't put it off long enough."

"You're so weird. Omegas are supposed to want kids. What happened to you?" I tossed my empty coffee cup in the trash receptacle nearby.

"We don't all need to be the same. You other omegas can have your babies and leave me be. I plan on fucking as many alphas as possible and traveling the world. You can't do that if you're in a committed relationship, or trying to drag snot-nosed brats around with you."

"Your take on motherhood is so heartwarming."

"Shut up." She snorted and punched my arm. "To each their own."

I sighed. "I just can't believe what an asshole that fertility doctor was. He was completely heartless."

"It's an odd job to be in if you hate kids."

"I'll say." I hadn't shared with her how the good doctor's touch had gotten me aroused. It was way too embarrassing. That little secret would go with me to the grave. "Plus, I spent a fortune going to see him and nothing changed. At least the other doctors were nice when they told me I couldn't have kids. He just acted like not having babies was a good thing."

"I know. Don't they teach doctors how to be compassionate?"

"He must have skipped that lesson."

"Well, either way, I think you're lucky you got away from Carlos. He was a jerk. He treated you like shit. You should have dumped his ass the first time you found out he'd cheated on you."

"I know. But it was hard. He was so cute, and he really wanted kids too. Some alphas are kind of stubborn about having kids young. But he was ready and willing."

"I'll say. He was so willing he didn't even wait for you. He went ahead and knocked up another omega."

"Very funny."

She smirked and glanced at her watch. "Crap. I really do have to go. You know I love you, right?" She leaned in and smacked her lips near my cheek.

"You'd better. No one else does."

"Pffft. Stop. Your mom loves you."

I winced. "Thanks."

She smiled and squeezed my shoulder. "I'll call you later tonight."

"Make it tomorrow. I plan on staying out really late."

"Remember what I said. Be careful. Use a condom. There are other reasons for that besides preventing pregnancy."

"I know."

She waltzed toward the door giving me a careless wave of her hand.

I went home and showered. Then I put on my tightest jeans and a fitted red shirt. I'd never had any trouble getting attention from alphas. I was blond and blue eyed, and that was like cat nip to most alphas. I knew I could find someone to fuck, but finding an alpha who wanted to be stuck with a barren omega would be a challenge. Not that I was looking for love tonight. Nope. This evening was all about sex. I needed to feel wanted. I craved hot, dirty club sex. No strings. Just pleasure.

I know eventually I'll have to settle down with an omega, and pop one kid out just to carry on the Hexton name.

Dr. Hexton's emotionless words came back to haunt me. How could anyone not want babies? I ached to fulfill my destiny, and yet I apparently never would, meanwhile, alphas like Dr. Hexton could get omega's pregnant, and he didn't want that. It was so fucking unfair.

I sprayed on some cologne and made my way to the club. When I arrived, the parking lot was full, and I ended up having to park on the street a ways away. By the time I hiked all the way from my car to the club, I was breathless and a little sweaty. The bouncer, Raul, knew me. We'd always had a little flirtation with each other, but he was older and he didn't touch younger omegas, so all we did was flirt.

"You going to behave tonight?" he asked, checking my ID like he'd done a hundred times before.

"Where's the fun in that?" I smiled, giving him a wink.

His lips twitched. "If I was twenty years younger."

"Oh, please. You're such a tease." I took my ID back from him and stuffed it in my back pocket.

"Yeah, you're right. Even if I was younger, I'd think you were too much trouble."

"Me? Trouble?"

He grinned and patted my backside as I moved past him. Maybe Dr. Hexton was right, and I just needed to find myself an older alpha who had no interest in having kids. Maybe Polly had it right too and traveling the world having fun was the way to approach life.

The club was crowded, and the music thumped through my body as I pushed my way between the dancers, toward the bar. As I neared the long bar, I was greeted by a few friends from work.

"You made it." My buddy Chip said with a grin.

"Nice shirt," Stewart said, eying me up and down. "You look mighty hot tonight, Mr. Johnson. Too bad we work together."

I laughed because Stewart and I were too good of friends to ever screw things up by sleeping together. Besides, it wasn't often omegas slept with each other. Occasionally, if you just needed to get off, it might happen, but mostly omegas were drawn to alphas.

Chip pushed a margarita into my hand. "Drink up. We know you need to let loose."

I sipped the drink and coughed. Waving my hand in front of my face, I grinned. "Jesus, is there any mix in here or is it pure liquor?"

"I think the bartender put a dash of lemon juice." Chip smirked.

"Thanks, guys." I lifted the drink.

"It's the least we could do." Stewart patted my back. "We know you've had a rough month."

As I drank the margarita, I eyed the guys nearby. There were some hot looking alphas in the club tonight; one red haired guy was making eyes at me, and there was another blond alpha I'd seen in the club before. When I locked eyes with one dark haired alpha about five feet away, my heart froze.

Dr. Hexton?

I started coughing like I was about to lose a lung, and set my drink down. My eyes burned as I wheezed and turned my back on him. What the heck was that uptight asshole doing here?

"You okay? Your face is kind of blue." Chip smacked my back.

I nodded, but couldn't speak yet. I prayed Dr. Hexton hadn't noticed how shocked I'd been to see him. But since I'd practically spit my drink out, odds were he'd been aware.

"Yeah, don't waste that booze. That drink was pricey." Steward nodded.

"Your concern is overwhelming," I whispered hoarsely.

Stewart just grinned.

When I peeked over to where Dr. Hexton had been, he was gone. Relief flooded me, and I even began to second guess whether I'd really even seen him. Maybe it had simply been someone who looked a lot like him. After all, the Wild Poppy Club wasn't really the sort of place I'd expect someone like Dr. Hexton to frequent. He'd probably hang out at higher end bars, where they could fawn over him as they served him caramel apple martinis.

By the time I'd downed two strong margaritas, I forgot all about Dr. Hexton. When the red headed alpha approached me to dance, I was more than ready to mingle. He was friendly, and he touched me a lot as we gyrated to the pounding music. My cock warmed as I held his lusty gaze, and when he pulled me close, and started nibbling my neck, I figured he'd probably be the guy I fucked tonight. He certainly seemed interested enough.

"I'm Peter." I slipped my hands down his sides and smiled at him.

"My name's Josh. I've seen you in here a few times before," he yelled over the music.

"Is that right?"

"Yeah. I've never had the nerve to approach you though."

I frowned. "Why not?"

"You had Carlos with you."

Distaste rolled through me. "Yeah. We're not together anymore."

He nodded. "I figured."

I didn't want to talk, or even think, about Carlos. I pushed closer to Josh and pressed my crotch against his. I was being way more aggressive than usual. Maybe it was because he'd mentioned my ex. It still hurt to think about Carlos dumping me just because I couldn't get pregnant. As if nothing we'd shared together had mattered, simply because I couldn't have kids? I'd been depressed and hadn't slept with anyone since he'd broken up with me. But I was done waiting for Carlos to come crawling back. I wanted to screw some other alpha and erase the memory of Carlos. I needed validation that I was still desirable, even if I was barren.

"Wanna go out back?" I licked my lips, hoping I looked sexy, and not just sweaty and nervous, like I felt.

Josh seemed kind of surprised at how assertive I was, but he nodded. "Fuck yeah."

"Let's go." I turned and abruptly slammed into someone dancing directly behind me. The force of the collision almost knocked me on my ass, but the person grabbed my arm and kept me upright. When I recognized Dr. Hexton in front of me, I winced, and pulled my arm from his grip. "Sorry," I mumbled, as the song ended.

He nodded. "No problem." His gaze flicked to my red headed friend.

"Well, anyways—" I started to move past him and he blocked my path.

"Can I buy you a drink?"

I scowled. "What?"

He made a drinking motion with his hands. "You know. Liquid in a glass. You swallow it."

"I know what a drink is. I don't know why you'd want to buy me one," I snapped. We hadn't exactly parted on great terms as I recalled.

"Awww, come on. Just one." He gave me a white smile, showing little dimples in his cheeks. "You'll hurt my feelings if you say no."

Who was this guy? The man I'd met a week ago hadn't bothered trying to charm me. I couldn't understand why he'd try now.

I lifted my chin. "No thanks."

His mouth drooped. "Why not?"

I scrunched my face in confusion. "Because me and my friend have other plans." I gestured toward Josh.

He glanced at the red head behind me. "I uh… I can buy you both a drink." He didn't sound thrilled about the idea.

"No thanks."

Josh shifted uncomfortably when Dr. Hexton settled his disgruntled gaze on him. "Are you two like… together or something?" Josh asked.

I scowled. "Hell no."

"Hmmm." Josh didn't look convinced.

Dr. Hexton's dance partner poked his head around the doctor's shoulder, looking annoyed. "Are we gonna dance or talk?" he asked.

Without even looking at the guy, Dr. Hexton said, "You should go find another dance partner."

Giving an unhappy huff, the omega hissed, "Rude!" And he stomped off.

Josh frowned, eying Dr. Hexton. "Um… Peter… maybe I should take off and let you two talk."

"No—" I began.

"That's a good idea," Dr. Hexton cut in. "I really would love to speak to Peter alone." His voice wasn't loud, but there was an authoritative quality to it.

"But I have no desire to talk to you. Stop trying to ruin my evening," I grumbled.

Dr. Hexton leaned toward me. "Let me buy you a drink."

My scowl deepened. "I believe I already said no thanks."

His eyes narrowed, and he repeated, "Let me buy you a drink, Peter."

I guess he thought adding my name on the end would make me obey, but I was just tipsy enough it didn't work. "My friend and I are going out back. I don't want a drink. I don't want anything from you."

Josh's uneasiness radiated off of him like a floor heater. "Um... maybe we should do this... you know... another time."

"What?" I gave him an irritated glance. "Why?"

Shrugging, the other alpha stepped away from me. "To be honest, the mood is kind of ruined." He flicked his gaze to Dr. Hexton.

I knew his uneasiness was because there were hierarchies within the alpha community. There was little doubt Dr. Hexton out ranked Josh. "You don't need to worry about him. I told you; we're not together."

Josh winced and shook his head. "Sorry, man." He turned and walked away.

I glared at Dr. Hexton as the younger alpha retreated. "Thanks a lot."

Dr. Hexton lifted one shoulder, looking pleased with himself. "You can do better than him."

"Is that right?"

"Yep."

"You and I both know that's not actually true."

He sighed. "Peter, you're overreacting to the… unfortunate news that I gave you. It's not like you're missing your head."

"Being barren is almost as bad."

"You're looking at it all wrong." He wrinkled his forehead.

"You wouldn't understand."

The music started up again, and a few of the dancers gave us irritable glances. Dr. Hexton seemed to notice, and he put his hand on the small of my back, and guided me off the dance floor toward the bar. I shivered at the feel of his warm fingers through the thin material of my shirt, and the memory of his intimate examination a week ago returned. My face was hot as I recalled how my body had responded to his touch, and I made sure not to look at him.

Stewart and Chip were nowhere to be seen as Dr. Hexton had me sit on the only available stool.

I gave him a pissy look. "Gee, what a gentleman," I grumbled.

His lips twitched, and he signaled the bartender. Even though it was a packed house, the guy came running over immediately. Dr. Hexton didn't bother asking me what I wanted. He ordered six tequila shots, and when the bartender went to get the drinks, he met my gaze. "We don't need to be enemies."

"We also don't need to be friends."

He sighed. "I'm not a bad guy."

"You're arrogant."

"I'm not." He frowned.

I looked at him like he was nuts. "Of course you are. You're also rude and insensitive."

"Not always."

I laughed gruffly. "And you're obtuse."

"In what way?" He truly looked perplexed.

"I was having a good time with my little ginger friend and you butted in." I scowled. "Why? Why did you butt in?"

"I wanted to talk to you."

I snorted and grabbed one of the shots when the bartender set them down. "I get the feeling you think the world revolves around you." I gave Dr. Hexton a dirty look, and I swallowed the tequila in one gulp. The liquid burned a little, and my eyes watered, but I simply licked my lips and ignored my unwelcome companion.

He swallowed one of the shots and then he leaned into me. "I don't like that you left my office mad at me. Most of my patients revere me."

"I find that hard to believe," I muttered.

"I have no control over the results I give you." He pulled his dark brows together. "You understand that, right?"

"It was *how* you delivered the news. I've had car mechanics who were gentler with me."

He licked his lower lip, looking puzzled, and unwelcome lust buzzed through me. Jesus, what was this weird sexual power he had over me? It was annoying as hell. I didn't want to notice how full his lips were, or how good he smelled. I didn't want to think about the feel of his fingers inside me; so firm and persistent that just thinking about that moment on his examination table could almost make me come.

Stop.

He drank another shot, and when he leaned into me, his heated, tequila infused breath made me shiver. "Okay, fine. I'm sorry."

His warm, husky words rippled through me from head to toe, leaving me confused. He annoyed the hell out of me, but there was something about him that also seemed to draw me in. But I didn't want to be attracted to him, so I clenched my jaw, and then drank a shot. We were so close; I could see the dark ring around his amber iris. His lashes were thick and long, and his gaze was intense. I could sense he was attracted to me too, and he also seemed just as confused by it.

"Do you forgive me?" He arched one brow.

I studied him, wondering why he cared if I forgave him or not. I knew I should tell him what he wanted to hear, if only so he'd leave me alone. Besides, it wasn't as if he'd run over my cat. He'd simply been obtuse in how he'd delivered some very bad news.

"Only if you change," I said softly.

He cocked his head. "Well, I have tried to be more sensitive since that day." He rubbed his chin, a line between his eyes. "Maybe because I deal with infertility all the time, I have become a little desensitized."

His introspective answer surprised me. "Well, maybe because it doesn't directly affect you."

He scowled. "You mean because it isn't all about me?"

I laughed gruffly. "No. I mean because you're an alpha and you'll be respected no matter what. We omegas have to earn our worth." I swallowed hard. "We do that by having babies."

He hung his head. "I keep telling you that isn't the only thing that makes an omega valuable."

"I know you do. But you're wrong."

He twisted his lips. "You know, Peter, I've listened to your critique of me. Maybe you should do the same."

"Oh, really?"

"Yes." He fingered his shot glass. "Omegas provide support for their alphas, with or without children in the mix. They stand beside us —"

"Don't you mean behind you?"

He scowled. "No. I wouldn't want an omega who stands behind me. I want a partner. Partners stand next to you, not in your shadow."

He sounded shockingly liberated. He'd seemed so overbearing and arrogant, and yet his take on the alpha omega relationship was downright enlightened.

"Do you actually believe all that?" I eyed him skeptically.

"Yes." He smirked. "Why do you think I don't have an omega?"

I rolled my eyes. "Oh, of course. I guess you've never met one that was worthy of standing beside you?"

He simply smiled and tossed back another shot.

When he'd finished his drink, it was hard not to fixate on his wet lips. My pulse spiked slightly when our eyes met. I pulled my gaze away and stared across the dance floor. Josh had found another dance partner already. I sighed, feeling frustrated that my plan for hot, meaningless sex had been thwarted by Dr. Hexton.

"So what exactly were you and your little friend planning on doing out back?" Dr. Hexton's curious voice cut into my thoughts.

I gave a stiff laugh. "Take a guess."

He frowned. "I don't really see you as that sort of guy."

"What sort?"

"The sex-behind-the-dumpster kind."

I scowled. "You know my blood type and that I'm barren. Other than that, you know nothing about me."

"I can guess."

"I doubt it."

He shifted, and his hip pressed against my arm. "I know that you don't want to lose your job, your alpha ran off with a fertile omega, and you don't forgive easily."

I gave him a sharp glance. "If I didn't forgive you, I wouldn't still be sitting here."

His features softened. "Really?" He sounded so pleased, it was hard not to smile.

"Why do you care what I think?"

He lifted one shoulder. "I'm not sure."

I shook my head. "You're an odd duck."

He captured his lower lip between his teeth as he studied me. His eyes were slightly dilated, and I suspected he was a little drunk. I was buzzed too, which was probably why I held his gaze longer than I should have. There was definitely mutual attraction between us. It was confusing though because I kind of didn't like him. Or at least, I hadn't when we'd first met. He was slowly growing on me. It took a lot for a proud alpha to apologize. I had to respect that he had.

"You're odd yourself," he said softly.

I didn't respond.

"Why were you going outside with that guy?"

I frowned at him. "Didn't we just go over this?"

"But I mean *why*?" He narrowed his eyes. "Is it to get even with your alpha?"

"He's not my alpha anymore," I growled.

"Right. But was that the reason?"

I inhaled and exhaled impatiently. "Why don't we talk about you some more? I'm sure you'd enjoy that."

He grinned. "I like that you're feisty."

I smirked. "You're aging yourself, Dr. Hexton. Nobody under the age of sixty uses that word."

"I'm only forty-five. And you should call me, Rafe."

"I'm not sure I'm ready to be on a first name basis with you just yet."

He sighed and eyed the dancers. "That's too bad."

"Is it?"

"Yeah."

I just laughed.

He cleared his throat. "So… do you still want to give the old fuck you to your ex?" He glanced at me, and if it hadn't been for the tension in his jaw, I'd have thought he didn't care about my answer. But that little tell gave him away.

"Well, unfortunately you chased away my little ginger friend."

"Yeah, but he's not the only alpha in the place."

I squinted at him. "Are you hitting on me?"

He pushed his tongue in his cheek. "No."

"Yes you are. You're hitting on me."

He grinned. "So what if I am?" He shrugged. "There's an obvious attraction between us."

"No." I shook my head, trying not to smile.

He narrowed his gaze. "Liar. I know you feel it."

"I don't like you."

"I'm not sure that's entirely true."

"It is."

He flared his nostrils, and a smile touched his lips. "I have a nose. I can smell your need."

My face warmed. "It's not personal. I'm simply horny."

"As am I." His eyes seemed latched on my mouth. "We have needs. Omegas and alphas have needs."

"Yes." My cock hardened as I held his gaze. He wasn't trying to hide his attraction now.

"We should help each other out."

"Is that right?"

"Physical need isn't anything to be ashamed of."

I shrugged. "True."

"Come home with me, Peter."

Excitement buzzed through me, but I tried to play it cool. It wasn't easy with my cock tenting my pants. "Why?"

A slow sensual smile spread across his lips. "You know why."

"Look, we're both a little drunk. This is just the kind of thing we'll regret in the morning." I tried to sound logical as I pushed away the memory of his fingers in my ass. My body betrayed me though, by tingling and warming at the recollection of his touch.

"I'm not asking you to marry me." He nudged me with his elbow. "It wouldn't be romantic. This would just be fucking. Dirty. Filthy. Fucking."

I swallowed hard as my nipples pricked at the lusty heat in his voice. "Wow."

"Does that scare you?"

"No," I said breathlessly.

He lifted one smooth brow. "Does that interest you?"

I met his amber gaze, and my stomach somersaulted at what I saw there. He wanted me bad. And as much as I'd disliked him when the evening began, I didn't feel that way anymore. In fact, I was pretty sure I didn't have it in me to turn down the chance to experience more than just Dr. Hexton's fingers in my ass.

I picked up the last shot, and I gulped it down. I coughed a few times, and with my eyes tearing, I said, "Yeah, Rafe. I'm definitely interested."

Chapter Two

We didn't even make it inside his house before he started kissing me. He pressed me up against the front door and took my mouth in a hungry kiss. His tongue probed deep into my throat, and his hands roamed my body; pinching my nipples and squeezing my ass. I moaned and kissed him back, aching to have him inside me.

When the kiss ended, I said breathlessly, "We're just using each other, right?"

He smirked. "Well, it ain't love."

I swallowed hard. "Okay." I wasn't even sure why I'd asked that. Maybe it was to let him know that I knew the score. I wanted him to remember that I wasn't some sappy omega who needed every alpha I fucked to become my boyfriend. My pride was pretty tattered after Carlos, and I didn't want to seem weak or desperate.

He glanced around at the neighboring houses. "Let's get inside." He released me, and his hands shook a little as he struggled to get the key in the lock.

I stood behind him, shivering in the frigid air. Once the door was open, he grabbed my hand, and pulled me into his house. My heart pounded as the door slammed closed behind us. His house was silent except for our heavy breathing. His eyes were an eerie yellow as he glanced back at me, his fingers digging into my wrist. I felt out of control with lust, and he seemed to be the same. Our inner wolves were most definitely in control at that moment, and nothing short of an earthquake would stop him from taking me now.

He pulled me down the narrow hallway, and I caught glimpses of family photos hung in perfectly straight lines. We entered his bedroom, and it was dark and warm. The moon shone through the sheer white curtains casting two white beams across his bed. He swung me around and walked me backwards, until the back of my legs hit the edge of the mattress.

His mouth came down hard on mine again, his tongue seeking. When he lifted his head, we were both breathless. He grabbed my shirt and ripped it open as buttons flew in all directions. Even though I loved that shirt, I didn't give a flying fuck at that moment. When he clamped his mouth on my beaded nipple, I groaned and unzipped his pants with trembling hands. He bit and sucked my nipples, and I moaned and wiggled against the painful pleasure.

My hand slipped into his underwear and wrapped around his thick cock. I pulled the stiff, heated flesh from the cotton cloth, my stomach clenching with anticipation at how fat his dick was. God, I wanted that inside me. I wanted him in me more than I wanted air. "Fuck me," I whimpered, gasping as he bit my nipple again.

"Don't worry. I will." He grabbed my waist and pulled me against him, rolling his hips. My hand was still clamped on his cock, and I rubbed my thumb over the seeping head. He moaned and undid my jeans too, shoving them to my knees. I hadn't worn any underwear because I'd figured it made quick hook ups easier, and I was really glad about that decision.

"Lube," I whispered. "In my back pocket."

He hesitated, and he looked almost insulted. "No underwear and lube. Jesus, you really were there to get laid."

"Yeah. Big surprise I came there to get laid. So did most guys in that place. And if you hadn't interrupted me, that pretty ginger in there would be inside me right now."

His mouth hardened. "Turn around." He knelt down, and rifled through my back pocket, then he tore open the packet of lube and stood. "Bend over."

I obeyed and closed my eyes, my heart banging against my ribs as I waited. His lubed fingers pressed against my hole, and then he pushed in, pulling a groan from my tight throat. "Oh, fuck," I whimpered, my cheek rubbing the soft satin comforter on his bed.

"You like that, don't you?" He leaned on my back, pushing his fingers deeper as he growled near my ear.

"Yeah," I groaned.

"Remember that day in my office?"

I nodded, hissing with pleasure. "I was so turned on."

"Me too. I just wanted to mount you on that table." He sounded breathless. "In fifteen years I've never been turned on during an exam. Never."

"Your fingers felt so good inside me."

"This tight ass was so tempting."

I frowned. "Of course, I also hated you a little."

"Is that right?"

"Yeah. You were an asshole to me."

"But you forgive me, right?" He laughed softly. "You want my cock, so you must forgive me."

"I'll let you know after you fuck me. Maybe you suck at that just like your bedside manner."

"Oh, really?" he grumbled.

"Yeah. Maybe." I smirked.

"You tell me, omega. Do I suck at pleasuring you?" He twisted his hand and rubbed my prostate, making me cry out and claw at the bed.

"Oh, shit." My body quivered as he worked my ass, pushing his finger in and out of me.

"You want me to leave you alone because I was mean to you?"

"No," I moaned, pushing back against his hand. "Fuck me."

"What did you say?"

"Shit. Fuck me. Fuck me."

He nipped the back of my neck, his hot breath making me shiver. "You want me to fuck you, omega?"

"Yes," I pleaded. "Fuck me now."

"I want you good and ready." He rubbed his fingers insistently, and I gasped and clenched my muscles on his hand. He chuckled. "You want this bad."

I could tell he wanted to tease me and draw this moment out. So I tried to think of things to say that might egg him on. "That other alpha wanted this ass. You know that, right? He wanted to fuck me outside up against a wall."

"Yeah?" he growled, pulling his fingers from my body. "Well, he doesn't get this perfect ass. I do."

"He had a big cock. I could feel it through his pants." I smiled against my arm when he huffed against my back. I started jerking my cock with one hand, wheezing, I was so turned on. I arched my back. "Pretty sure he'd have been a good lay."

"Enough." His voice rumbled in his chest. He rubbed the slick head of his cock over my hole, up and down, teasing me. "Feel that? That's *my* dick, omega. That other alpha backed down because I'm the superior alpha. Do you understand that?"

"I know you think that."

He gave a grudging laugh. "I'm sure you'll agree when my cock claims this tight hole of yours."

"Then what are you waiting for?" My legs shook I was so ready. "Fuck me, alpha. Take what you want."

With a grunt, he pushed in, and I saw stars. The pressure was incredible as his thick cock rammed into my tight channel. I cried out, and bit my lip so hard I drew blood. The pleasure mixed with pain as my muscles stretched to accommodate his width.

"Fuck, you're tight. Oh, fuck." His voice shook, and he started giving little thrusts until he was fully seated in my hole.

I moaned, but my cock went semi-limp because my ass ached from his size. I felt stuffed full of him and my entire body throbbed.

But then he started slowly rolling his hips, and everything changed. "Yeah, that's right. Let me in. Let me fuck you deep."

The friction of his cock inside me coaxed loud groans from me as it began to feel amazing. I squeezed my eyes shut and started stroking myself. My cock hardened again and filled with blood as he flexed his hips back and forth quicker. "Oh, god," I hissed. "Fuck me. Fuck me harder."

He bent his legs and started thrusting upward, pounding into me like a machine. The bare slide of his flesh inside me had me shivering and moaning like a French whore. At one point I realized he didn't have a condom on. I'd had one along with the lube in my pocket, but he'd obviously ignored that rubber, and just rammed into me bare. We hadn't addressed whether we'd use a condom or not. It wasn't as if he'd ignored my wishes. But just knowing he'd needed to be in me bare, made everything ten times hotter. Maybe I should have said something. I knew better than to bareback an alpha I hardly knew. But for some reason I didn't care. He'd said this would be dirty. Filthy. Fucking. And he'd been right. As he screwed me deeper and deeper, I was so turned on that he was doing it raw, I couldn't stop my climax, and I came. I came so hard my legs gave out, and I would have collapsed if he hadn't held me up. Streams of cum rippled against the sheets as my muscles clenched with an intensity I'd never experienced.

"Oh, my god," I groaned, shuddering and quaking with pleasure.

He wrapped both arms around my waist and started fucking me harder, in and out, in and out, and then he came too. A hot flash of seed filled my insides and trickled down my inner thighs. He growled and kept fucking me until his cock eventually softened inside me. Breathing hard, he pushed me against the bed and we both collapsed, breathing like race horses. He kissed the back of my neck affectionately, with his cock still buried inside me.

After a while he grunted, pulled out, and stood. I slowly twisted around, still using the mattress to prop me up. "My god." My legs still felt shaky and weak. "That was fucking intense." I smiled weakly, feeling breathless.

His eyes were a darker gold now. "Was I too rough?"

"Hell no." I shook my head.

He grinned and walked into what I assumed was the master bath. I heard water running and then he came out carrying a towel. He tossed it at my head and I grabbed it mid-air. I wiped myself and the comforter off, and stood, feeling incredibly relaxed.

"Well, doc, thanks. That was a nice ten minutes." I laughed, admiring his long lean legs and beautiful buttocks. He certainly wasn't shy about walking around naked. Nor did he have any reason to be.

He grimaced at my comment and pulled on his underwear. "I usually last a little longer. But I've been fantasizing about that nice ass of yours for a while now." He moved up to me. "Sorry I didn't use a condom. Um… I got a little carried away."

I bit my lip. "Yeah… well, we didn't discuss it, and I didn't try and stop you."

"True." He studied me. "But I should have asked."

I gave a gruff laugh. "Neither of us were thinking straight."

"No."

"At least we know I'm not pregnant."

Wincing, he touched my cheek. "I'm sorry I was insensitive to you that day in my office."

I dropped my gaze to his Adam's apple. "It's okay."

"Not really. That's not the kind of doctor I want to be."

I was surprised by the gentleness of his tone. "Then I guess you can change that."

His smile was slow. "I'm gonna try."

"Good. Your patients will thank you for it."

"I'm sure you're right." He hesitated. "You know… you don't have to bolt out of here."

I studied his face, uncertain if he was just being polite, or if he actually wanted me to stay. "It's late."

"True. But it's Friday." He frowned. "Do you work tomorrow?"

"No."

"What exactly do you do?" He sat on the edge of the mattress.

"I'm a buyer for a men's wear store."

"Really?" He winced and glanced around. "Shit. I destroyed your shirt."

I shrugged and pulled on my briefs. "It was worth it. I can probably get another one. They just came in last week."

"I'll buy you a replacement."

I frowned. "No need."

He twisted his lips as he watched me. "Don't want an alpha buying you things?"

"I can take care of myself."

"I've no doubt. But isn't it nice to get gifts?"

I bent over and grabbed my pants from the floor. "Depends who's giving them I guess."

With a gruff laugh, he said, "I'm not sure how to take that."

I ran my gaze over his beautiful body, lingering on his muscled thighs and groin. "I don't need gifts. I enjoyed fucking. But I didn't plan on seeing you again."

Lifting one smooth brow he said, "Oh, really?"

"Yep."

He smirked. "Well, in all fairness, you didn't plan on fucking me either."

I laughed. "True."

He stood and moved closer, his musky scent filling my nostrils. "We don't always control all the twist and turns of life."

My lips twitched. "You should be a motivational speaker."

"Sure. If this famous fertility specialist thing doesn't pan out, I'll think about it."

I grimaced. "Jesus, you really are kind of a celebrity in this town. I keep forgetting that."

Shrugging, he said, "It's a very small town."

"You're well known outside of Poppy Field too. I saw you on TV last month more than once."

"True." His dimples appeared.

"I guess I should feel honored you felt bad about a little nobody like me. So bad you wanted to fuck me and make it all better."

He frowned. "You know, I really did feel bad. It's not my fault you turn me on."

"I know. It's mutual."

"After you left my office last week, I kept thinking about you." He gave a puzzled laugh. "I truly have never been attracted to a patient before. It was very odd."

"I've been examined many times, and all I wanted was for it to be over." I sighed. "I was so afraid you'd notice I had an erection."

"I didn't. I was too busy praying you didn't notice mine." He put his arms around my neck, his gaze focused on my mouth. "I think you should definitely stay the night."

"Is that right?" My stomach clenched with excitement at the salacious look in his eyes.

"Yep. Especially if you don't plan on ever seeing me again. This might be my only chance at that gorgeous ass of yours. I'd like to prove I can last over ten minutes."

"I should have known it's all about you protecting your delicate alpha pride."

He leaned in and kissed me, pushing his tongue between my lips, and tearing a whimper from me. When he lifted his head I was breathless and clinging to him. God, he did something to me. It was scary how much I wanted him.

"Stay." His voice was husky.

I pressed closer to him, my cock hardening against his. "Like I have a choice."

Beau Brown

Chapter Three

Stewart's eyes were wide. "I'm sorry. You had sex with that asshole, Dr. Hexton?"

I sliced open a box of new arrival shirts with my cutter and tucked it away in my pocket. "It was a one-time deal."

"And that makes it okay?" He shook his head. "That's almost worse."

I straightened, rubbing my back. "Why?"

"Because you let him use you."

I scowled. "We used each other if anything." I pulled some shirts from the cardboard container. "What's the big deal, anyway? You, I and Chip were there Friday to get laid. Mission accomplished."

"But that guy made you feel like crap when you had an appointment. It took you a week to stop moping around." He leaned against the storage room door, looking annoyed. "How could you have sex with him? I thought you hated him."

I scowled. "I didn't hate him. I thought he was rude. But he apologized."

"Sure. So he could get in your pants."

Facing him, I put my hands on my hips. "Are you going to do any work today, or am I on my own?"

He pushed away from the door, still scowling. "I didn't take you for a pushover."

"Jesus, Stewart, how many times do I have to tell you it was just sex? He's not a bad guy once you get to know him out of the office."

He shook his head and pulled a glittery black tank top from the container. "It's just hard to keep it all straight. One minute you loathed the guy, now you love him."

"Love him?" I bugged my eyes. "I don't love him. Are you crazy? We fucked. That's it. I was out to have a good time, and he obliged."

"Whatever." He held the tank up to himself. "What do you think?"

I gave him a grumpy glance. "I think that would look amazing on you, and from your pissy attitude this morning, I'm guessing you didn't get laid Friday night or this weekend."

Stewart's face fell. "There were a couple of guys at the club who were attractive, and they seemed interested." He sighed. "But I just wasn't feeling it."

"You used to love picking up guys. What's gotten into you lately?"

He slipped the black tank top onto a hanger. "I think the baby-bug is finally hitting me."

I gasped. "No way."

He slumped, giving me a depressed look. "I don't know what's going on with me. I used to love being free and easy. Now all I can think about is settling down with an alpha and maybe having a kid or two."

I felt a twinge of envy. "Well, you won't have any trouble finding an alpha if that's what you really want. You're good looking and you can have kids." I glanced down at my stomach forlornly. "Me on the other hand."

Stewart moved closer and patted my back. "Kids aren't everything."

I winced. "Said the guy who literally just confessed he can't wait to have kids."

Grimacing, Stewart's cheeks tinted pink. "This is what happens when I try to console my friends. I end up making it worse."

I forced a laugh and went back to unloading the clothing from the box. "Nah. I'm fine. I'm just trying to focus on the good part of not having kids. For example, I could go on vacation tomorrow if I wanted, without having to either drag a screaming baby with me, or arranging childcare."

"Very true."

"I can drag sexy alphas back to my place and screw their brains out, without worrying about waking up a kid. I'm the center of my own life, not a supporting role." I swallowed hard, trying to think of other perks of being childless. "I don't have to change dirty diapers, or wear pureed peas on my clothing just because Jr. wasn't in the mood for veggies that day."

"Absolutely." Stewart gave a weak smile.

I exhaled and met his gaze. "I simply have to get used to the idea that a family just isn't in my future."

"Or you can adopt."

"Yes. But I don't know many local agencies that are gung-ho to give a kid to a single omega who can barely pay his rent." I made okay money, but I'd never been good at saving, and so I didn't have much to show for it. I rented a house and drove a nice car, but I didn't have much left over at the end of the month.

"If… if it's something you want, I'm sure you can make it happen." Stewart's voice was falsely bright.

"In the meantime… my life is full." *Sure. Me and my parakeet Fluffy are living the dream.* I turned away from my friend so he couldn't see my depressed expression. I'd come to terms with my situation sooner or later. I just needed a little more time.

When my phone buzzed in my pocket, I pulled it out and glanced at the number. I didn't recognize it immediately, and so I didn't answer it. Stewart and I went back to putting out the new spring collection, and when lunch rolled around, we split a small veggie pizza next door at the Italian restaurant.

By the time it was five, I was more than ready to head home. The nagging depression from my earlier conversation with Stewart hadn't waned. I just wanted to go home, put my feet up, and have a few beers. I let Stewart leave, and I finished counting the till and straightening the cash wrap. I'd been lazy about locking the front door, so when the bell rang, and someone walked in, I sighed and prepared to give them the speech about being closed.

When I recognized Rafe, my stomach flip-flopped with excitement. "Oh, it's you." My voice wobbled, and I was annoyed I didn't sound confident. But I hadn't expected to see him again, and certainly not at my work.

"I'm in need of a few casual shirts for a weekend trip I have coming up." Rafe smiled, his amber eyes bright with obvious attraction.

My pulse raced as I smiled tentatively at him. "How did you know I worked here?"

He twisted his lips. "Who says this isn't a chance meeting?"

I laughed nervously, my body tingling as he came closer to me. "I don't picture you as our target demographic."

He frowned. "What does that mean? Are you calling me old?"

"No. But not counting parents shopping for their teenage kids, most of our customers age out at twenty."

He grabbed his chest and scowled. "You wound me, sir."

I couldn't help smiling, and he looked pleased. His dark blue shirt fit his muscular torso perfectly, and he smelled great. In fact, he looked so fucking good I felt nervous around him. I wanted to ask him how he'd found me, but I didn't know how to broach the subject without it sounding accusatory. But I was curious because I definitely suspected he hadn't stumbled into my store by accident.

He leaned on the cash counter. "I've been thinking about you a lot since Friday." His husky voice sent shivers through me.

"Is that right?" I'd been thinking about him too, although I'd tried not to. I'd told him I didn't plan on seeing him again, and I'd meant it. But then the memory of how nice it was to be fucked by him had lingered, and I'd regretted my hasty decision.

"Have you thought about me?" He looked and sounded supremely confident, but there was the slightest hint of apprehension in his pretty eyes.

Glimpsing that vulnerability softened me, and I nodded slowly. "Hell yes."

Tension left his jaw. "I'm glad. I wasn't sure. You seemed pretty definite you didn't want to see me again."

I fiddled with a label gun near me, to distract myself from his intense stare. "I should have said I don't *usually* see guys again. Not when we just meet at a bar."

"So then it's not like a rule of yours?"

"No. Not really." I laughed gruffly. "Honestly, most guys I hook up with I wouldn't want to see again."

He gave me a cocky smile. "But I'm different, aren't I?"

I shrugged. "We don't only know each other from the club."

"That's true." He smirked. "We have a history."

"Yeah, a history of you pissing me off."

He winced. "Now don't go getting all mad at me again. I prefer it when you like me."

Grinning, I moved past him to lock the shop door. I didn't want any other people wandering in. Not when it seemed like maybe Rafe and I had some things to discuss. I was excited, and flattered, that he'd sought me out. When I returned to him, I didn't bother going behind the cash area. I stopped near him and pretended to straighten some shirts on a rack nearby.

He cleared his throat. "So I was wondering if you wanted to grab dinner, and then maybe go back to my place?"

"Are you buying?"

"Of course."

I stopped pretending to work, and I faced him. "You want to fuck me again, don't you?"

He licked his lower lip. "Duh."

I laughed. "Not even going to pretend you're here for any other reason?"

He moved closer, slipping his hands around my waist. "Why bother?"

My cock immediately filled with blood at his musky scent. I shivered at the hungry look in his eyes, and I dropped my hands to his hips. "You gonna fuck me bare again?"

His eyes sparked with lust. "Yes."

My stomach somersaulted with need. "I shouldn't let you."

He pushed me slowly up against the cash wrap and whispered, "But you will, won't you omega?"

My hunger swelled inside my gut and I moved to slowly unzip his pants.

I could sense his surprise, but he didn't put up a fight. His breathing picked up, and he slid his hands to my ass. "I jerk off every morning thinking about this beautiful ass of yours. I can't stop thinking about how tight you were."

"Yeah?" I was glad he wasn't wearing a belt because once I had his zipper undone, I could easily reach in and grab his stiff cock. "I jerked off this morning thinking about this monster. I want more. I want so much more."

He let out a little growl, and he moved to undo my jeans. Excitement rumbled through me as I let him yank my pants and underwear down below my knees. I stumbled back into the counter, and he followed. His eyes were light yellow and salacious. "Turn around."

I smirked. "No. I want to look in your eyes when you fuck me."

He didn't look annoyed, in fact, he smiled. "Sounds good to me. I want my tongue down your throat when I fill you with my seed."

I whimpered against my will, my omega responding instinctively to him breeding me. *If only.* As he shoved his pants down to his ankles I watched him, my ass aching for what was about to happen. He straightened and then put his hands around my waist. He lifted me onto the counter and he stepped closer. "I really planned on buying you dinner first," he panted.

"After." I sounded breathless. "You can feed me after you fuck me, alpha." I spread my thighs, my cock ruddy and stiff.

He pulled me forward, so that my ass hung off the edge, and he spit on his fingers. I assumed that meant he didn't have any lube with him, and I sure as shit didn't keep any at work. When he slid two fingers into me my ears rang, and I arched my back.

"Oh, shit," I gasped, pleasure mixing with discomfort.

He watched me closely, pulling out and teasing my hole gently. "Yeah, loosen those muscles." His voice was low and his eyes heated. "I can't wait to slide in this sweet hole. Shit, your ass is like a vise on my hand."

I whimpered again and put my arms around his neck. "Feels nice," I whispered. I wasn't lying, now that I'd relaxed my clenched muscles, it felt way better. Good even.

He worked me softly, deftly, kissing me and nibbling my jaw. "I've thought of little else." He pushed his fingers deeper, stroking over my prostate.

I shivered and groaned, rolling my hips and trying to fuck myself on his fingers. "Oh, god, Rafe. Do it. Fuck me."

He pulled his hand away, his eyes glittering with need. "Yeah, I need to be inside you." He pushed my thighs wider, and moved in, pushing the wide head of his cock to my puckered hole. The mushroom shaped head of his dick was slick with pre-cum, and I hitched a breath in my tight throat when he pushed in.

I threw my head back and cried out with pleasure. The pressure was intense as he slid in, and I shuddered as I took him deep. "Oh, fuck," I hissed, clutching him and digging my fingers into his arms.

He growled and flexed his hips, thrusting back and forth, his lips parted. "So good." He adjusted his position to where my legs hung over his forearms as he pounded into me. "Goddamn, I needed this. Needed this so bad."

"Me too," I moaned, squeezing my eyes closed as the pleasure buzzed and nipped at my swollen balls.

He leaned in and kissed me, and our tongues tangled with lust. He sucked at my mouth and I did the same back. We were like hungry animals as we took what we wanted from each other. He continued to slide his cock in and out of me as we locked lips. I'd never been with an alpha that could seem so gentle even as he pounded my ass. He was a real mixture of lustful and nurturing. Instinctively, I knew he wouldn't hurt me. He was passionate but thoughtful, and my eyes almost rolled up in my head it felt so damn good.

I was thankful we had tinted windows that made it impossible for anyone to see into the shop, not without being right up against the front glass. What an eyeful anybody would have had if they'd bothered to glance in. The sound of flesh slapping and heavy breathing filled the little clothing store. Sweat rolled down his cheek as he continued to fuck me, and I held his gaze, feeling transfixed by his yellow eyes.

His thrusts slowed at one point, and it just felt even better. His cock slid deep and slow, coaxing ragged groans from me. "Oh, yeah. Right there, Rafe. Fuck. Fuck." My muscles shook from the strain of holding myself in the awkward position on the counter. But I wasn't moving until I got my release. No way. Firemen could have burst into the place, and I'd have just told them to fuck off until I came.

He rolled his hips, and his fingers sank into the skin of my thighs. "Come for me."

I started jerking myself, holding his gaze. "Yeah? You want to fuck me until I come?"

"Yeah." His movements sped up. He leaned in and kissed me again, and I wound my legs around him, moaning into his mouth.

The pistoning motion of his hips, and the delicious friction of his dick inside me, shoved me toward the edge. I squeezed my cock and clenched my ass on his shaft, needing to come desperately. My climax started at the base of my cock, swirling through my balls, and snaking up my cock. His jagged movements stuttered, and I felt his dick swell inside me.

I shuddered and came, and he did too. With his tongue down my throat, and his cock buried deep inside my ass, he shot hard. I grunted and wiggled beneath him as he continued to thrust deep, filling my hole. Every inch of me flushed with heat and pleasure, and eventually he stopped moving and just held me. We shivered against each other, breathing hard and kissing softly. I didn't quite understand what it was about him, but his scent and touch drove me nuts.

He pressed his lips to my throat, giving a breathless laugh. "Shit. I just lose control around you."

"I'm not complaining."

He pulled out, and I grabbed a box of tissues we kept on the counter for customers. As he wiped off, he gave a wary glance at the cameras around the shop. "Did we just put on a show for your boss?"

I laughed. "No. Those are dummy cameras. The lady who owns the place is too cheap to shell out the money for a real security system."

He blew out a long breath. "Good." He helped me down off the counter with a grin.

Once we were cleaned off, and redressed, I asked, "Did you really need shirts?"

Looking a little sheepish, he shook his head. "Not really. But I'd have bought a few if that was the only way to get you to talk to me."

I laughed. "Well, I won't insist you buy anything now. That would feel way too weird to make a commission off of you after having sex."

He smiled. "You ready to go to dinner?"

Frowning, I switched off the lights and led the way to the front door. "That's not necessary. I can just grab something on the way home." I assumed the offer of dinner was about as real as the need for shirts.

He pulled his brows together as he stepped out onto the sidewalk. "I actually want to have dinner with you, Peter."

I finished locking the door and faced him. The scent of honeysuckle hang thick in the balmy spring air. "But you don't have to do that."

"I planned on eating with you." He almost looked annoyed. "Do you not want to have dinner with me?"

I grimaced. "I'd love to. I just didn't think that was actually the plan."

"You thought only sex was?" He laughed. "Well, I understand that since I practically pounced the second the door was locked."

"I'm… I'm happy to eat with you. What kind of food do you want?"

He surprised me when he put his arm around my shoulder and steered me toward his car. "Anything you want."

"You're mighty agreeable, Dr. Hexton."

"It's the new me." His Mercedes chirped as he unlocked it.

I frowned. "Why don't I just drive my own car and meet you there?"

"We can talk on the way if we ride together."

I laughed, mostly because I didn't think he was interested in me for my conversational skills. But when he opened the door, I slid in willingly. I was flattered he deemed me worthy of dinner and not just sex. He could probably have had dinner with any omega he wanted.

I watched him as he got in the car, and when he glanced over and gave me a warm smile, my gut fluttered. I was puzzled by why he seemed so interested in me, but I was enjoying getting to know him better, so I decided not to worry about it.

Chapter Four

"This is fun, right?" Rafe's teeth were white against his tanned face. His hair ruffled in the sea breeze as he handed me a glass of champagne. "Fresh air and sun on our faces. Doesn't get better than this."

"This is amazing." He'd invited me out on his yacht for the day. I'd been surprised when he'd called because every time we saw each other for the last two weeks, I'd assumed it would be the last time. Neither of us was looking for a relationship, or at least that was what we both said. But time after time he kept calling or showing up, and I kept accepting his invitations.

"Ever dated anyone with a yacht before?" He arched one smooth brow.

"Hell no."

He grinned. "I didn't think so."

"Why? Because no one with a yacht would usually be with someone like me?"

"No, that is not what I meant. But you seemed really excited when you saw the boat. It made me think this was a new experience for you." He sipped his drink, studying me over the rim.

I inhaled the salty air. "Carlos wasn't in the same tax bracket as you. He didn't have a boat. He did rent a canoe once when we went to the mountains." I made a face. "But it had a hole in it, and we sank in the middle of the lake after about ten minutes. I should have known then that was a bad omen."

He chuckled. "We won't sink."

"I have no doubt."

"Captain Phillips has a perfect track record."

"I'm sure you wouldn't hire anyone who wasn't perfect. Like you."

"Very funny."

I smiled.

He cleared his throat. "Carlos… that was the name of your alpha? The one who ran off with another omega?"

We didn't usually talk about personal stuff, so I was surprised when he asked about my ex. "I wish he'd truly run off. Unfortunately he's still in town."

"That's awkward."

"Tell me about it. I ran into them in the grocery store the other day. They were kissing on the diaper aisle."

He frowned. "How fitting, considering he sounds like a piece of shit."

I laughed at his protective tone. "Shouldn't you be on his side? Don't all alphas stick together?"

"Hardly. He sounds like a douche."

I grinned. "Oddly enough, those were on that aisle too."

His eyes were warm as a slow smile spread across his handsome features. "I like hanging out with you."

"Do you?"

He nodded. "It's surprising."

I frowned. "That tactful remark sounds a lot like the old Dr. Hexton."

"Oops. What I meant was simply that we had a rough start."

"That we did." I sipped my champagne, staring out across the azure sea. "Thank you for inviting me today. I really needed to get outside and clear the cobwebs."

"I'm glad you said yes." He sighed. "Glad, and also surprised."

"Why?"

Shrugging, he said, "I keep expecting you to reject me."

"Me too."

He laughed.

I grimaced when he refilled my champagne flute. "That's probably enough for me. I don't want to get drunk."

He snorted. "Drunk. Sober. You'll end up in my bed either way."

My gut tumbled with anticipation. "You're pretty sure of yourself."

"I just know you're as attracted to me as I am you."

"Yeah." Why lie? It was obvious he turned me on. I stretched my legs out, getting more comfy on the deck chair. The sun was warm and soothing as it sank into my skin.

"So tell me a little about Carlos."

I winced. "Seriously?"

"I'm curious about the man who would be dumb enough to dump you."

"Ouch. I prefer to think it was mutual."

He frowned. "Was it?"

"No." I snorted a laugh. "But I prefer to think it was."

He nodded. "Got it. You like to lie to yourself."

"I guess."

We sat in silence for a few more moments and then he asked, "So come on. Tell me about this mysterious Carlos."

"He wasn't really mysterious in any way." I shoved down my distaste at thinking about my ex. "He was emotionally distant. But not mysterious."

"What does that mean; emotionally distant?"

I scrunched my face, trying to find the words to describe Carlos. "He said all the right things, but his actions didn't really support them."

"Ahhh. Yeah, I get that."

"Once he found out I couldn't conceive…" I winced. "He made me feel like I was an ugly scarf he was stuck with."

He scowled, his amber eyes bright with irritation. "It's not your fault. How dare he blame you."

"He really wanted kids. I guess I can't condemn him for not wanting to be with me forever. I couldn't give him what he wanted most."

"I've never been in love... but I'm pretty sure that isn't how it's supposed to work. You're supposed to stick by each other through thick and thin. Right?"

"That's what all the Reese Witherspoon movies tell us."

"You don't bail the second you run into a problem."

I shrugged. "But he really wanted to have kids. Are you saying you'd have stayed with a barren omega? Or an omega who couldn't give you the thing you wanted most?"

He considered my question, a line between his eyes. "I think I would. If I love someone, I'm very loyal."

"But you've never been in love. You just told me that."

"I have *loved* people though. I just haven't had that great romantic love. But I adore my parents and siblings. I'd do anything for them."

I couldn't help it, and I laughed. When he scowled, I said, "I'm sorry. It's just so weird to think of you as caring about anyone."

The line between his eyes deepened. "Why?"

"I don't know. You seem very in control of your emotions."

"I am in control of them, but I do still have feelings."

"I guess you seem aloof."

"Aloof?" He widened his eyes. "That's a horrible word."

"Why?"

"Well, because I'm not. I'm actually very warm when you get to know me."

My lips twitched. "I'll take your word for it."

His cheeks seemed flushed. "You don't think I'm warm?"

If I was honest with myself, he was incredibly giving during sex. "I suppose you are when it suits you."

"Your tone implies I'm only nice to get what I want."

"I don't know you well enough to be passing judgment. I shouldn't have said anything."

His disgruntled gaze held mine. "To be honest, *you* seem aloof, when I think about it."

"Pfft. Is that right?"

"Don't you want to know why I think that?"

"Why?"

"Because you supposedly loved Carlos, and yet you talk about him like he's a gardener that didn't work out." He looked smug. "What do you think of that?"

Maybe his opinion irked me because there was a hint of truth to it. There'd been times when, even I'd wondered, if I was with Carlos simply because he was convenient. After all, he'd been sexy, eager, and there. Even though he'd only been twenty-two when we'd met, his drive to procreate had been as strong as mine. We'd shared that desperate drive to have kids, and although we'd tried for a year to conceive, it hadn't worked. "I guess you and I are both heartless assholes." I kept my voice emotionless.

"Perhaps." He tipped his glass and finished off his drink. "Maybe that's why we seem to mesh so well. We have no expectations of each other."

As the boat cut through the sparkling water, I shifted when my stomach twinged slightly. It wasn't a rough sea by any stretch, so I wasn't sure why I suddenly felt a little queasy. Maybe it was the champagne combined with the motion of the boat that was getting to me. I'd never been on a boat before, and it was possible I simply hadn't adjusted to the movement yet. I'd always been a wimp when it came to roller coasters too.

"Well, either way, it's Carlos' loss," he said.

"Thanks." I winced as my stomach rolled again. I hadn't eaten much for breakfast, maybe that had been a mistake. Would I feel better if I'd had a large meal?

"You're not drinking." His voice was curious. "This is expensive bubbly. I wanted to give you a treat."

I rubbed my stomach, grimacing. "I'm not feeling my best."

He frowned and sat straighter. "Really? You should have told me."

"It snuck up on me." I closed my eyes, trying to let the cool breeze and warm sun soothe me. I jumped when he touched me. When I opened my eyes, I found him knelt beside me, looking concerned.

The touch of his hand on my wrist gave me even more butterflies. "Would you like to lie down? Maybe that would help settle your stomach."

"I'm sorry. I'm ruining everything."

"No. Not at all. I just want you to feel better."

I swallowed, the queasiness increasing. "Do you think perhaps you could point me in the direction of the bathroom?" I was mortified. I couldn't believe Rafe had invited me onto his magnificent yacht, and I was about to humiliate myself by spending the day in the toilet, barfing.

He stood and held out his hand. "Come on." I grabbed his fingers, and he pulled me to my feet. I swayed against him, and he slipped his arm around my waist. "It's okay." His voice was soothing, and I was impressed he didn't seem worried about me puking on him.

He led me down a narrow stairway to where the cabins were, and he stopped in front of one of the doors. "This is the bathroom. Take your time."

"Thanks." I went into the restroom, heading straight to the toilet. I didn't even stop to lock the door I was so desperate. I leaned on the porcelain bowl, sweat breaking out on my face. I couldn't understand why such a calm day at sea had my stomach so upset. But it was, and as a wave of overpowering nausea hit, I emptied the contents of my stomach.

A half hour passed with me vomiting, and hanging onto the toilet, feeling like I was about to die. Eventually, the sickness seemed to fade away, leaving me weak and shivering. I sat on the tile floor, leaning against the sink cabinets, breathing hard. I just wanted to curl into a fetal position and sleep. I hadn't been this sick since I was in college and I'd over indulged at a keg party.

There was a soft knock on the bathroom door, and it slowly cracked open. "Are you okay, Peter?"

I just groaned. I really didn't want him to come inside the bathroom, but I didn't have the strength to tell him to stay out. I stayed where I was, staring at the door as it opened wider. Rafe frowned when he saw me, and he rushed over.

Kneeling down, he touched my sweaty cheek. "Shit. You're white as a ghost."

I licked my lips and groaned again.

He stood, and grabbed a wash cloth from a rack, and then he wet it, and returned to me. He softly dabbed my cheeks and forehead. It felt nice, and I closed my eyes, grateful the horrible nausea had slipped away.

"You should lie down." He rose and then gently grabbed me by my arms. He managed to get me upright, without much help from me.

My mouth felt gross. "Toothpaste."

"What?" He laughed, looking at me like I was crazy.

"My breath is horrid. I want to brush my teeth." I swayed, and he gripped me tighter. "Please."

He looked around the bathroom. "This is the guest bathroom. I don't think there's anything in here." He brightened. "I have breath mints." He propped me against the counter and dug in his back pocket with one hand. He pulled out a plastic container of mints. He shook one tablet out and put it against my lips.

I sucked it into my mouth and whispered, "More."

He frowned. "Why are you worried about your breath at a moment like this?" But even though he complained, he gave me two more mints.

I grunted my thanks, swirling the peppermint tablets in my mouth with relief. As soon as I felt better, I was determined to hunt down a toothbrush.

He shook his head as he tucked away the mints. "You're so weird."

I nodded, still sucking on the candies.

He smiled and helped me from the bathroom. I expected him to lead me back up on deck, but he didn't. Instead he took me down the hallway to a bedroom. I knew immediately it was his room because it smelled like his masculine cologne. The drapes were closed, and the room was dark and cool. We stumbled over to the bed, and he had me sit on the edge. He unbuttoned my shirt slowly, and then he pulled it off. Next he pushed me down on the mattress and went to work undoing my pants.

I mumbled something unintelligible, but he ignored me. He pulled off my shoes and tossed them aside, then he tugged my jeans off and pulled back the covers. I was so exhausted I didn't argue. I crawled into the sheets and sighed when he tucked the soft blankets around me.

He sat on the mattress and stroked the hair off my forehead. "Now you just rest, okay?"

I didn't respond, keeping my eyes closed. I couldn't remember anyone ever really taking care of me when I was sick like this. It was a nice feeling to be nurtured and valued. I snuggled into the sheets more, and he chuckled.

"We can spend the night on the boat, so there's no rush. I was hoping to convince you to stay over anyway." His voice was husky.

"I'm sure this wasn't how you saw the day ending," I whispered, feeling guilty.

"Shhh." He continued to stroke my hair gently. "I like taking care of you."

I didn't know if that was true or not, but I was too tired to try and figure it out. Instead I sighed, and allowed myself to drift off into a wonderful, deep sleep.

Beau Brown

Chapter Five

When I woke, it was nighttime. A warm body pressed against my back and there was the sound of a soft snore every few seconds. My lips curved in a smile as I realized it had to be Rafe sound asleep in the bed with me.

I felt rested, and my gut was no longer queasy. I needed to pee, so I slowly pushed back the covers and got out of bed. I tiptoed across the big cabin toward the bathroom area. Once I'd used the toilet, I washed my hands and grabbed the tube of toothpaste I spied. I felt too weird using his toothbrush, which was probably ridiculous, considering we'd had sex many, many times. But I used my finger to brush my teeth instead.

Then I got back in the bed, facing Rafe. His breathing was shallow now, and I had a feeling he was awake. Even so, when he spoke I jumped. "How are you feeling?"

I gave a self-conscious laugh. "Much better."

"I'm glad."

I grimaced. "I'm sorry about ruining the day."

He turned toward me, his features hard to see in the dark. "Don't be silly."

"I had no idea I'd get seasick."

"Next time I'll give you Dramamine before we get on board."

"You mean after an awesome day like today there will be a next time?"

"Yes." His voice was still husky with sleep. "I told you, I like hanging out with you."

He'd been so kind to me earlier, I felt immense gratitude. "It's mutual."

He moved closer, and I was finally able to see his face better. "I hated not being able to help you." He frowned. "I don't know if that's the doctor in me or the alpha."

"Maybe it's a little of both." I tried not to read too much into Rafe's nurturing behavior toward me this afternoon. Alphas were driven to comfort and protect omegas. They almost couldn't help it. Occasionally you got a bad apple like Carlos, who put their own needs first. But generally, alphas took care of omegas.

I didn't complain when he slid his arm around my waist and pulled me against him. His cock was hard against my thigh, and a curl of lusty need swirled in my groin. He smelled so good and his body was warm, and fit into mine perfectly. But he didn't make any move to have sex. He just held me and kissed my hair, inhaling deeply. It was the oddest thing to be held by an alpha for any reason other than sex. I couldn't remember ever being this close to an alpha that they didn't try to get inside me. I waited for him to make a move, but he didn't.

Had I turned him off by being sick earlier? Maybe I grossed him out now. As he held me, all sorts of insecure thoughts rolled around in my head. I reassured myself that if he didn't find me attractive, his cock wouldn't be stiff like it was. Maybe he was just being considerate by not making a move.

After a while, he let go of me, and rolled onto his back. "I wanted to ask you something."

"Okay."

He turned his head to look at me. "What do you think about how much we've been hanging out together?" His voice was soft and inquisitive.

"I've enjoyed it."

"Me too." He sounded breathless. "Are you… seeing other alphas?"

His question surprised me. He actually seemed almost nervous asking me that. Was he seeing other omegas? I wasn't sure I wanted to know if he was. That thought surprised me too. He'd made me no promises, and I had no reason to think we were exclusive. But I really liked him, and the thought of him with anyone else irked me.

When I didn't answer right away, he said quickly, "Never mind. That's not really any of my business."

I searched his face in the dim light. "I don't mind you asking. And no, I haven't been seeing anyone but you."

Tension seemed to leave his jaw, and he sighed. "Okay."

What about you?

That inquiry hung frozen on my lips. If he said yes, he was seeing other omegas, it would bother me. Not only because I'd let him bareback me, but because the thought of him giving another omega the attention he gave me felt weird. Part of the problem was that when he was with me, he had a way of making me feel as if I was the only omega in the world. I'd never had that before. Most alphas I'd dated had openly admired other omegas in front of me. It had always bugged me, but Carlos had told me that was just how alphas were. They couldn't help wanting other omegas too. Since Carlos had been my only serious relationship, I'd believed him.

"This thing between us... it's taken me by surprise," he said quietly.

I wasn't exactly sure what that meant, so I wasn't sure how to respond.

"I know it's not my place... but I feel... possessive of you." His voice wobbled.

A weird excitement lit inside me. "Yeah?" What did that mean? What was he trying to say?

"From that first day in my office, something about you got to me," he mused. "I thought it was just physical at first." He laughed. "And it is that too."

"It's only been a couple of weeks. I'll probably start annoying you soon." I still felt confused about what his point was. I assumed he had a reason for asking if I was seeing anyone else. "I'm most charming in small doses."

"I don't agree. I truly enjoy your company. I feel like I understand you, and so your quirks don't bother me. I know you get pissy when you're insecure, but I don't care. I'm learning that when you get really quiet, I've usually said something stupid."

"You're a blunt person."

"Yes. I need to work on that."

I gave a gruff laugh. "Who the hell are you, and what have you done with Rafe?"

He sighed. "That's kind of what I'm saying. Being around you has affected me. Changed me."

I was in shock at how forthright he was being about his feelings. But it gave me enough courage to ask the burning question I wanted to ask. "So… are you seeing other omegas?" I hated that my voice broke on the end of the sentence. I cringed, waiting for his response.

He hesitated, and then he said, "I was going to, after that first night, just because we'd both made it clear we weren't looking for anything serious. But instead, I spent the entire weekend alone, wondering what the fuck was wrong with me." He laughed. "I had no desire to call anybody like I usually would. But I didn't have the nerve to call you either."

"You had the nerve to show up at my work on Monday."

"Yep." He shifted uneasily. "I was glad you were receptive."

"Very receptive as I recall. Every time I ring up a customer I get turned on now."

He chuckled and then fell silent. "Maybe we're a good match."

My pulse spiked at his soft words. "Meaning what?"

He turned to face me, and he sat up on one elbow. "You can't have kids, and I don't want kids."

I stared at the ceiling. "As you well know, I don't generally see my being barren as a good thing."

"I'm trying to spin it in a positive light, but yes, I know that upsets you."

"I still don't know what you mean by 'we're a good match.'"

"Just what I said, you can't have children and I don't want them."

"I thought you said you would eventually need to... let's see... how did you put it? 'Settle down with an omega, and pop one kid out just to carry on the Hexton name.'"

"Oh, god. Did I actually say that?"

"Yes. Yes you did. You also told me I had a better chance of being hit by a meteor than getting pregnant." I gave a stiff laugh. At first, his words had hurt, but enough time had gone by and the pain had faded. It was also easy to forgive him because he looked and sounded horrified.

He groaned. "I'm so sorry. Jesus. I tend to get really wrapped up in the clinical side of things. I find the study of infertility fascinating. But of course that's a horrible thing to say to someone."

"It was crushing."

He put his hand behind my neck, and he pulled me in for a kiss. His warm mouth felt nice against mine, and I sighed. He smiled against my lips and then lifted his head. "Please forgive me for being an asshole."

"Okay." I grinned.

His expression was watchful. "Should I continue elaborating on my theory of us?"

"I guess." He had an entire theory of us? What was he trying to say? He definitely had me intrigued. Half the time I couldn't understand why he was spending time with me. In his position, he could most likely have any omega he wanted. Yet he'd admitted to only seeing me the last two weeks.

"I'm sure what I'm about to say will come out of left field for you." He gave an uneasy laugh.

"I won't know if you never tell me."

He exhaled. "Well, I've been mulling an idea that I think would be mutually beneficial to both of us."

"Okay." Was he ever going to actually give me any details?

"As you well know… it's not good for an omega to be alone."

It was true that most omegas in our alpha omega society, were expected to be coupled with an alpha and pregnant by the time they were in their twenties. "Maybe a normal omega shouldn't be single. But I don't think the usual rules apply to me because I'm barren."

"You're still an omega. You still need the support and love of your alpha."

Love.

We both seemed to stiffen at that word.

He laughed awkwardly. "I'm not saying we're in love." He gave another forced laugh. "But I think we're a good pairing. We get along well, and sexually there's no doubt we're compatible. We would make an excellent match."

My pulse sped up as I grasped what he might be suggesting. "You want to be my alpha?" I sounded breathless.

"Well, why not?"

I frowned. "You'd want to be stuck with an omega that can't carry on your family name?"

"I've thought about that. If all I want is an heir, we could always adopt or perhaps use a surrogate. That child could still carry on the Hexton name."

"But you don't want a child."

He chuffed. "No. I do not. But I feel the same pressures you do about procreating. Especially as the eldest in my family. We each have our roles. However, I also have a younger brother named Jaden, and he really wants kids. He could carry on the bloodline, so it's not all up to me. Unless something awful happened to Jaden, I don't need to have kids."

"Well... um..." I didn't know what to say. He'd obviously given this lots of thought, which was surprising. The whole time we'd seen each other I'd expected him to get bored and move on, but here he was suggesting we become permanent mates.

"I know this is sudden." He sighed. "You probably think I'm nuts."

"Not nuts... but it is a shock."

"Yeah. The thing is, I really like you." He sounded puzzled. "I don't meet many people I like spending time with. But being with you isn't work. I can be myself, and you actually seem to enjoy me too."

"I do like being around you. I wouldn't have seen you again if I didn't."

"That's what I figured. And every time I ask, you say yes. That seems to confirm you feel the same as me. Plus, just like you'd have trouble finding an alpha who wouldn't want kids, I have the same problem finding an omega that is cool with not having babies. It goes both ways."

I hadn't really thought about that from his point of view. He was right, omegas self-worth was tied up in having babies. That was one reason I'd struggled so horribly with not being able to have kids. But none of that would matter to Rafe. In fact, my being barren was a plus in his book.

"Wow. I don't know what to say." My voice was soft.

"We'd both benefit from this arrangement."

I squinted at him. "You'd really want to be saddled with an omega who can't reproduce?"

"Absolutely. I told you, I don't need or want kids. I really dislike the noisy little rats. And I completely disagree with your theory that your sole reason for existing is to have babies. That's sheer nonsense. You're an amazing person. I'd be lucky to have you as my omega."

My face warmed. "Many alphas would say you're crazy."

"Well, they're wrong."

I felt a little overwhelmed at his unorthodox suggestion. It had certainly caught me by surprise. "I won't lie; this is the last thing I ever thought you'd propose. I wasn't even sure you'd want to keep seeing me at all, let alone this."

He touched my cheek. "I can't stop thinking about you. I'm almost embarrassed to admit that to you. But you truly do occupy way too many of my thoughts. And when I imagine you with another alpha, it brings out the oddest territorial feelings in me. I'm not familiar with these jealous emotions. I've never wanted to keep an omega to myself."

"I'm afraid you'd come to regret your decision."

"No. I wouldn't. I can admit I'm lonely sometimes. Don't you ever feel lonely?"

My face warmed. "Of course."

"Well, why should we be alone, when we like being with each other?" He smiled.

"Maybe Carlos has made me gun shy." I bit my lower lip, feeling confused.

He nodded. "I get it. You've been hurt. I'm sure because of a lot of the things I've said you see me as this confirmed bachelor type."

I gave a gruff laugh. "Yeah, kind of."

"I'll admit it was fun to fuck around when I was younger, but I'm forty-five now. I like the idea of having one omega who knows me and likes me. And having you share my bed... well that's just about the best gift I could give myself."

I almost couldn't believe what was happening. Rafe was rich, accomplished and sexy as fuck. And he *wanted* me. He wanted me knowing full well I could never get pregnant. When would a chance like this ever come along again? Especially with a man like Rafe. But it all felt very sterile and businesslike. Was that really what I wanted?

He must have sensed my internal struggle. "Peter, this isn't as cold as it sounds. I do have feelings for you." He touched my hand. "I think about you all the time. I wonder what you're doing when you're not with me. I worry about you, and if you're happy. I find you witty and intelligent, and obviously I find you ridiculously attractive. If I'm ever going to settle down, you're exactly what I'd want. So it occurred to me... why wouldn't I snap you up?"

He sounded so earnest it was impossible not to believe him. "It's just scary."

"I understand. But as I told you, I'm very loyal. You'd never have to worry about me cheating on you and leaving you for another omega. You'd be taken care of the rest of your life, and in turn, I'd have the companionship I crave, but without the pressure of having to impregnate my omega."

If I said no, would I spend the rest of my life alone, shunned by alphas in search of fertile omegas? The thought of that gave me a stomach ache. I didn't want to live alone, watching others living their lives. I wanted to have a happy life too. Maybe sometimes I acted tough, like I didn't need anybody, but I wanted to be cared for, and adored as much as any omega did.

"What do you say?" His voice was guarded. "Shall we be become mates? Who needs kids? Not us."

My heart ached at his flippant words. The thought of not having babies was crushing. Maybe he'd change his mind in the future and we'd adopt. He'd said that might be a possibility. Perhaps I really could have it all if I just took this chance with Rafe. I really did like being around him, in spite of how we'd met.

I nodded slowly. "Okay," I whispered.

"Really?" He didn't sound like he quite believed me.

"Yes." I spoke more firmly.

He smiled and pulled me close. "That's wonderful. I'm so glad."

I molded into him, my heart banging against my ribs. I was excited and terrified. But taking this journey with Rafe seemed better than living my life alone. Finding love wasn't easy. Most alphas weren't my type to begin with, and when you narrowed that group down by which ones wouldn't care if I could have babies or not, the pool of available alphas shrunk even more.

Rafe gathered me in his arms, and his heart beat beneath my ear. I knew my friends and family might think I'd lost my mind, but just being in Rafe's embrace soothed me. I decided to focus on that, instead of all the things that could go wrong.

Little did I know how fate was about to screw with me.

Beau Brown

Chapter Six

As suspected, Stewart and Chip thought I'd lost my mind by moving in with Rafe, but my mother was thrilled. She'd worried I'd never find an alpha because of my "condition" and so she was over the moon happy for me. She'd dropped by one morning to lend me moral support, as I moved the rest of my clothes in to Rafe's house. Rafe was at work, so it was just me and my mom.

"This house is gorgeous," she said, nodding at me approvingly. "Who'd have thought you'd snag such a rich, handsome alpha?"

"Thanks, mom."

She laughed. "You know what I mean. I prayed every night you'd find someone, but I really didn't think you would."

"Again, thanks."

"Come on. Don't go getting all sensitive on me." She perched on the edge of the mattress, smoothing her hand over the silk comforter. "Rafe seems nice."

"I like him."

"I've never known you to date an alpha older than you. You seemed to prefer party boy types." She smiled. "Maybe you're finally growing up."

"He's got more to talk about than the typical losers I dated."

"Speaking of losers, how is Carlos?" She smirked.

I grinned. "Nice one."

"He was always such a clod. I never really understood the attraction." She stood and looked around the room. "Can I help you put anything away?"

"I'm pretty much done. That was the last box. I gave all my furniture to the Goodwill. It was all second hand crap anyway. I just brought my clothes and Fluffy."

She sniffed. "Birds are disgustingly messy. I hope Rafe doesn't get annoyed with Fluffy's chirping night and day."

"He likes her." I winced. "I should say he tolerates her."

"And he really doesn't want kids?" She lifted one smooth blonde brow. "It's not just an act?"

"Why would he pretend? He didn't have to lie about that to… er… sleep with me. There would be no reason to lie."

She covered her ears. "I don't need to know about the sex stuff."

I laughed. "He wouldn't have asked me to be his omega if he wanted kids. Right? He's the one who told me definitively that I was barren."

"True." She hesitated. "Have you met his family yet?"

"No."

"What's the hold up?"

I frowned. "I just moved in yesterday. We've only been dating four weeks. I'll meet them when the time is right." I tore the tape off the box and folded the cardboard flat. Then I tucked it away in the closet. I suppose I should have thrown it, but a part of me didn't really believe Rafe could want me permanently. I guess my insecurities were what made me tuck the box away in case I needed to move out in the future.

"Did you want to go grab breakfast? My treat?" She hooked her purse strap over her shoulder.

My stomach gurgled at her suggestion, but it wasn't from hunger. I felt slightly nauseated and wasn't sure why. In fact, I'd been feeling a bit under the weather the last two weeks. I'd never really fully recovered from when I'd been sick on Rafe's boat. I assumed my weak stomach was caused from the stress of moving in with my new alpha. "I'll keep you company. I could use coffee."

She frowned. "You don't want to eat? You look a little thin."

"I know. I think I have a stomach bug. I've lost a few pounds, but I'll put it back on." I led the way downstairs.

We took my mom's car, and once we'd arrived at the Eggs and Stuff Cafe, she ordered a big breakfast, and I got coffee and some plain toast. She filled me in on her life at the Poppy Field Senior Apartments. My dad had died six years ago, and my mom had sold the house and moved into that complex a year later. She'd hated living alone, and she had lots of friends and activities to keep her busy now. I was glad she seemed so happy because I did feel a little guilty that I didn't always make time for her. Maybe now that I'd found my alpha, my life would be more settled.

When the waitress brought the food, the sight of my mother's fried eggs made my stomach roll. I clenched my jaw, fighting against the nausea that attacked me. I was getting tired of this strange sour stomach that seemed to come and go without a reason.

"Do you feel okay?" My mother frowned at me.

I grimaced and stirred cream into my coffee. "I'm fine," I lied.

She didn't look convinced, but she shrugged and broke one egg yolk with her fork. The sight of the oozing orange yolk made my gut heave. I stood quickly, rattling the silverware and dishes on our table, and bolted for the men's room. I made it just in time, and I dry heaved into the toilet, feeling sweaty and weak.

What the fuck is wrong with me?

I stayed in the restroom for a while, trying to suppress the feelings of nausea. Eventually the sickness faded, and I stood on shaky legs. I splashed water on my face and rinsed my mouth. Then I rejoined my mother who looked worried.

"I was about ready to barge in there and check on you." She leaned toward me. "How long have you been feeling sick like this?"

I sipped ice water and then wiped my sweaty cheeks with my napkin. "It started the day I went on Rafe's yacht. That was when it first hit me. But ever since then it just attacks me randomly throughout the day."

She narrowed her eyes. "Huh. Do you think you had food poisoning maybe?"

"I don't know. I don't have any other symptoms of that. It's just my stomach."

"Is there any particular time of day that it hits?"

I sighed, leaning back against the booth. "It seems worse mid-morning. But it bothers me in the evening now and then." I made sure not to look at her plate. I felt a little better and I wanted it to stay that way.

"You should definitely see your doctor."

"I live with a doctor now."

"Right. But does he know you still feel sick? Or does he think it was just that day on his boat?"

I did usually try and hide my stomach issues from Rafe. I'd assumed it was just a bug, and it would pass soon. It had been easy enough to keep my problem from him since I'd still been at my own place. But now that I'd moved in, if I continued to feel sick, it would be hard to hide. The only reason I hadn't told him was I didn't want to be a burden the minute I moved in. I was usually in really good health, so throwing up all the time was embarrassing.

"How about I drop you off at Rafe's office?" She put her credit card on the tray with the bill, and the waitress whisked it away.

"No." I scowled. "He's a busy man. I can't just show up expecting to get an appointment."

"Honey, you're his omega. You're not just some patient off the street." She laughed, looking at me like I was crazy.

"I know… but he's really booked solid all the time. It took me months to get an appointment with him the first time." I really didn't want Rafe to feel like I was taking advantage of him. "I'll take a nap and an antacid and I'm sure I'll be fine."

My mom didn't look convinced. "Anything that goes on longer than two weeks isn't good, honey. I'm serious. I'm taking you to Rafe."

My face was hot. "No. That's embarrassing."

Her jaw hardened. "He's your alpha. He's supposed to protect you and look out for you. He'd be mad if he knew you were hiding this from him."

"You're wrong. He doesn't need to know about this."

"Well, I'm telling him. You won't, so I will."

"What?" My voice squeaked. "No. You can't do that."

She took her card back when the waitress brought it, and she stood. "I can and I will. You're my son and I'm worried about you. Rafe would want you to come to him."

"I live with him now. I can just talk to him about this tonight."

"Pfft. Please. I know you too well. You won't bring it up. Besides, he won't have his equipment at home. You should have a blood test or a urine test. How's he supposed to examine you at home?"

"Mom, you're overreacting."

"I'm taking you to his office." She had a stubborn set to her chin, and I knew my mom well enough to know I wasn't going to win this battle.

I sighed. "Fine. But you'll see, he's so busy he won't be able to see me today."

She widened her eyes. "What kind of an alpha wouldn't make time for his own omega?"

I didn't know how to explain to her that we had a rather unusual sort of arrangement. My mom believed that Rafe and I were in love, and I let her think that. Why not? It made her more accepting of our relationship that way.

I followed her out of the diner. We were both silent on the drive over to Rafe's clinic. I was nervous he might be mad or impatient with my mom. She'd only met him once, and she'd been on her very best behavior. Today I had a feeling she would be her usual pushy self, and I wasn't sure how Rafe would react to that.

The waiting room was full, but the receptionist still greeted us with a smile. "Hello, do you have an appointment?" she asked, shuffling papers around on her desk.

"Um..." I grimaced.

"Hi, you don't know me," my mother began. "This is my son. He's Dr. Hexton's omega, and he really needs to be examined."

My face felt like it was on fire as I met the surprised gaze of the receptionist.

She laughed nervously. "Oh, um... I didn't know Dr. Hexton had an omega." I got the distinct feeling she didn't really believe my mom. She probably thought my mother was some batty old broad who just wanted to cut the line. I couldn't blame her.

"We can just come back another time—"

"Oh no we can't!" My mother interrupted me. "Can you maybe buzz the good doctor, and ask him to come out and speak to us?"

Oh, my god. Please let the ground open up and swallow me whole.

"No. Please don't bother him. I'm fine. I can talk to him at home." I could feel the eyes of everyone in the waiting room on me. How had I let my mom talk me into this? Why hadn't I walked home instead? A twenty mile walk would have been better than this humiliation.

When the door to the waiting room opened, and a nurse called out a patient's name, I caught a glimpse of Rafe walking down the hallway. He held a clipboard, and he was frowning. But when he glanced up, our eyes met, and the smile that lit his face made my gut tumble. He looked so happy to see me it was a shock.

He came toward us, looking surprised but pleased. "Hey," he said as he reached me. His gaze was warm. "This is a nice surprise." His gaze shifted to my mom. "Hello again, Mrs. Johnson."

She wagged her finger at him. "I told you to call me Silvia." Her smile softened her words.

Rafe smiled at us, looking curious. "What brings you here?"

"It's nothing—" I began.

"Don't listen to him." My mom sounded annoyed. "He's been sick to his stomach for two weeks, and he doesn't want you to know because he doesn't want to bother you."

If it was possible, my face felt even hotter as Rafe turned his muddled gaze to me.

"Is that true?" he asked, looking confused.

"It's no big deal." I shifted uneasily.

"You've been sick to your stomach for two weeks?" The line between his brows deepened. "Why didn't you tell me?"

I shrugged. "I'm sure it's nothing."

He scowled. "Viral gastronenteritis symptoms usually last just a day or two." He rubbed his chin. "Occasionally they may persist as long as ten, but it's rare."

My mom's expression was smug. "See there? Gastron-whatever-you-call-it should only last a day or two."

"But he said it could last ten." I defended.

"Not usually." Rafe chewed his lip. "Come with me." He took hold of my elbow and pulled me toward the door off the waiting room.

"I'll just wait out here," my mother called after us.

I gave her an exasperated glance and let Rafe drag me into an examination room. He closed the door. "Sit on the table please and take off your shirt." His voice was brisk.

I frowned, but I did as he requested. The air in the room was chilly against my bare skin, and I shivered. He came closer, and he put his stethoscope to my chest. I flinched but didn't say anything. I couldn't tell if he was annoyed with me or not. His face was blank, and I didn't know his expressions well enough yet.

"Breathe in," he said curtly.

I did as requested.

"Now out."

I blew out a long breath.

He met my gaze, and his expression told me nothing.

"I'm sorry to bother you at work. My mom just insisted. I'm really sorry." He could probably hear how fast my heart was beating with that stethoscope pressed to my chest.

He lowered the instrument and his mouth was a hard line. "Why didn't you tell me you've been sick?"

"It just comes and goes."

"That's a non-answer."

I shrugged.

He turned his back on me and opened a drawer. Then he pulled out two syringes, gauze, alcohol swabs and collection tubes. He set them on a tray and rolled it over to me. "I'm going to draw some blood. Just to be sure."

"Is this really necessary?" I frowned.

"Yes. I want to check your electrolytes and blood cell count. Then we'll do a urinalysis for dehydration and infection." He washed his hands at the sink as he spoke, then he dried them and pulled on gloves.

"Oh, geez. This is all so silly."

"No it's not. I can't believe you've been sick for two weeks and you didn't even mention it to me." He huffed. "In fact, you hid it from me." He tied a tourniquet on my arm as he spoke. "Unbelievable."

"Don't be mad."

"I am mad. As your alpha, I'm supposed to take care of you. How exactly do I do that if you hide shit from me, Peter?" His eyes were bright with irritation.

I hated that he seemed upset. It made me feel weird, and I just wanted him to stop glaring at me. "I'm sorry. I didn't want to be a pain in the ass before I even moved in."

His mouth was a grim line. "Bullshit."

Surprise fluttered through me. "What?"

He rubbed a spot in the crook of my arm and lined the needle up with the vein. "You didn't trust me."

I opened my mouth to speak, but instead bit my lip at the pinch when he inserted the needle. I waited until he'd drawn my blood and removed the needle. "Didn't trust you about what?" I asked.

He pressed cotton to the injection site and then covered it with a bandied. When he was done, he put his hands in his white coat pockets and studied me. "I said I'd be loyal. I said I'd stand by you. But you don't believe me, do you?"

I swallowed hard, dropping my gaze. "I believe you."

"Liar."

I glanced up, surprised. "Rafe, I believe you're a good alpha."

"Really? Then why, the first time you had a problem, did you hide it from me? Do you think I'm so shallow I'd bail on you just because you're sick? Is that how little you think of me?"

Sighing, I said, "I hadn't even moved in yet. I didn't want to be a pain in the ass before we'd even begun. Besides, I'm sure it's nothing."

He sucked in a big breath and exhaled, as if trying to calm himself. "Look, I like taking care of you. Whatever is making you sick is probably just a virus. But I want to be sure. I want you safe. And most importantly, I don't want you to be afraid to come to me if you think something is wrong."

I pressed my lips together feeling relieved he cared, and embarrassed I'd been so untrusting. "I'm not used to alphas like you," I said quietly. Carlos had hated problems. He'd never been there for me when I'd needed him. I guess I'd become accustomed to keeping my issues to myself. "I'm sorry."

He shifted uneasily. "It... it's okay."

I flicked my gaze to his and caught a flash of hurt feelings. My heart squeezed at that vulnerable glimpse into him. "I'll do better."

He sighed and stepped closer. "I'm not Carlos. It took me forever to commit to an omega, but trust me when I say, I won't let you down. Okay?"

I nodded, feeling a lump in my throat.

"This is new for both of us, and it will take a little adjusting. But I think it's worth it." He hesitated. "Do you still want to do this?"

I studied his tense face. I didn't want to stop seeing him, and he'd offered me an amazing chance at a normal life. I was excited about having him as my alpha, even if I was a little unsure of how to trust completely. "I wasn't hiding stuff because I don't want to be with you. I hid my illness because I *do* want to be with you."

He gave a gruff laugh, and he leaned in and kissed me. I wound my arms around his waist, and kissed him back, grateful he was his old self again. When he lifted his head, he smiled, and

Chapter Seven

"I'm beat." I walked into the house feeling like I'd run a marathon. It was inventory at the shop, and I'd worked fifteen hour days the whole week in preparation.

Rafe was on the couch with his feet up, reading. He lifted his head and smiled. "Welcome home."

I peeled off my hoodie and hung it on the rack near the door. "You look relaxed. Must be nice."

He frowned. "It's my one day off."

I came closer, and he moved his legs so I could sit on the sofa with him. Excitement rippled through me as I met his gaze. I still had to pinch myself every day that he'd wanted me as his omega. "I'm just teasing." I smiled.

"I've warned you before about teasing me." His voice was suggestive.

I laughed, and my pulse ramped up. "So what did you do to amuse yourself all day?"

He sighed. "Let's see… I slept in till noon, then I had toaster waffles for lunch, and after that I don't think I've moved from this spot."

"Sounds nice."

"It was." His eyes warmed. "It would have been nicer if you'd been here too."

"Well, somebody has to pay the bills." I grimaced because we both knew my income was a drop in the bucket compared to his.

He chuckled. "Yep." He put his sock feet on my lap. "Do you want to cook tonight, or shall we just order in?"

"Let's order in. I'm too tired to do anything. Well, anything that requires standing."

He licked his lips. "I'm glad you clarified."

I laughed at his insinuating tone. "You seem frisky and ready for action."

"I'm always ready for action. With you."

"Same." I gave him a shy smile.

I'd officially been living with Rafe for a week now, and so far we got along great. He'd been careful with pushing for sex too often because I still felt under the weather. The blood and urine test results were due back either today or tomorrow, and I was a little concerned that I still didn't feel right. I could just tell that something was off. My feet were often swollen, and I had lots of headaches. But true to his word, Rafe had never been anything but supportive and kind. He never made me feel guilty for not feeling well.

He sat up and set his book on the coffee table. "What kind of food are you in the mood for?" He studied me as he spoke. "How's the stomach today?"

I grimaced. "I felt queasy at work this morning, but better as the day progressed."

"How about now?"

"I feel pretty good. Tired. But not nauseated."

"I told Clarisse to call me if the results of your tests come back today." He glanced at his watch. "It's after seven though, so odds are it will be tomorrow."

"Yeah. I'm conflicted about the tests."

"Why?"

"Part of me wants them to find something, so we can fix it, and part of me is afraid they'll find something that's really bad."

Like, I'm gonna die, bad.

"Nah."

"But you don't know that because you have no idea what's wrong with me."

He sighed and patted the couch. "Come closer."

I hesitated, but I liked being near him, so I had no objection to getting close to him. He was mostly reclined, and he moved so that there was room beside him. I scooted between the back of the couch and his long, lanky body. He put his arms around me, and I rested my head on his chest. I exhaled and let his soothing alpha energy sink in.

"Better?" he asked softly.

I nodded, my cheek rubbing against the cotton of his shirt. "Yes."

"It's going to be fine. You seem really healthy in every other way. If you had some horrible disease, it would be manifesting in more than one way, probably.

Probably.

"I'm not usually sickly."

"Exactly. That's what I'm saying. If you're generally in good health, it's probably nothing. I mean, if you were vomiting blood, well then, yeah, I'd be worried." He stroked my hair as he spoke, his voice rumbling under my ear.

It felt wonderful in his arms. Carlos had never just held me. But Rafe did that kind of affectionate gesture all the time. At first it had sort of felt awkward for me because I wasn't used to it. But now I loved it. I even looked forward to when he got home after work. Often we'd sit on the couch and just vent about our day. He was a much better listener than I'd suspected, and I always felt better after sharing stuff with him.

"You never talk about your family." His tone was hesitant.

I sneaked a peek at his face and found him watching me. "That's because we didn't have that kind of relationship at first. I thought we were just fucking."

"Okay, but now you know it's more. You're my omega and I should know about your life and your family." He kissed the tip of my nose.

I laughed. "I had no idea you were this person."

He frowned. "What person?"

I sat up on my elbow, smiling at him. "You're so nurturing." I shook my head. "Sometimes it's hard to reconcile that you're the same guy whose office I stomped out of only a month or so ago."

He shrugged. "You're also more vulnerable than I'd have suspected."

"I guess we didn't really know each other."

"Nope." He narrowed his eyes. "We still don't. Which is why I want to learn more about you."

I lay down again and fiddled with a button on his shirt. "My dad died when I was eighteen."

"I'm sorry."

"He was a great man. I loved him so much. It almost killed my mom when he died. They were best friends. She had to sell the house because she couldn't stand being there without him. It was too hard."

"I can see that. If your life was completely intertwined with someone, and then suddenly they're gone, it would be a hard adjustment."

"She's much happier now, but it was really rough the first two years." My mother had been an absolute wreck after dad had died. I'd tried to be there for her, but I'd been grieving myself, and hadn't wanted to cry in front of her too much. She'd needed my strength, not my tears.

"What did he die of?"

"He died in a car accident. Just a freak thing and he was gone." I swallowed, trying to hold back the depressing memories that wanted to grab hold of me. My father had been the best alpha I'd ever known.

"That's awful." He tightened his grip on me.

"He was a great father and man. He'd drop anything to help anybody. There aren't a lot of alphas like him to be honest, and he'd have hated Carlos with a passion." My laugh was raspy.

He was quiet for a while, and then he asked, "What do you think he'd have thought of me?"

I considered his question carefully. "I think he'd have liked you if he met you away from your office."

He laughed. "Am I that bad at work?"

"You're very focused. When I met you that night at the club, it was like you were a different person."

He nodded, and I was relieved he didn't seem insulted. "I'm glad you gave me a second chance."

"Me too."

He cleared his throat. "Are you enjoying being here with me?" There was an endearing wobble in his voice.

I hid my smile. "Yes."

He slid his hand down my hip, to cup my ass. "I'm certainly enjoying having you here."

"Yeah?"

"Something tells me you know that."

I inched my fingers down his stomach and stopped just short of his crotch. "I'd had a feeling, yeah."

"I'll be honest; I wasn't sure I'd like having someone in my house." He gave a stiff laugh. "I was worried we might get on each other's nerves."

"Same."

"But so far, I love having your companionship... and all the other stuff too."

"It's kind of like a one stop shop."

He chuckled. "I think I definitely picked the perfect omega for me. I wanted a no drama relationship, and I've got that with you."

"I hate drama."

"I can tell." He caressed my back absentmindedly. "My mom wants us to go over for dinner soon."

My stomach clenched with nerves. "Oh... um... okay." It wasn't like I could avoid meeting his family forever.

"Are you nervous?"

"Hell yes." I laughed. "What if they don't like me?"

"They will. You're very likable."

"Do they know anything about me?" I glanced up at him. "They don't think I'm a doctor, right?"

He smiled. "No. They know you're not in the medical field."

"But do they think I'm as accomplished as you?" I didn't know many families that would be happy their son the doctor had settled with a buyer at a clothing store.

"My mom is just happy I finally picked an omega."

"Yeah, but do they know I can't have kids?" I winced. "That might color her opinion of me big time."

"Her main concern for me was companionship." He tightened his grip on me. "I've found that. She'll be happy for me."

"Will your brother be there and your sister?" The thought of meeting everyone at once seemed daunting. But maybe it was better to get it over with at once. Just rip off that Band-Aid.

"I'm not sure. She simply said she wanted you to come to dinner one night soon."

I shifted uneasily. "Would you say your family are easy going people? Or are they serious?"

He chuckled. "I'd say they're easy going."

"Okay." I blew out a nervous breath. "Good."

"As I said earlier, my family wants me happy. If we seem to be a good fit, they'll support us."

"Are your brother or sister dating anyone?"

"Not seriously."

"Okay." I nodded. "Maybe that's better. Then there's no one to compare me with."

"You'll do great. Should I set the dinner up for next week?"

"Sure." I fake gulped. "Maybe I'll get lucky and the test results will say I'm dying. That would be a good excuse to cancel, right?"

He scowled. "Don't say stupid things like that."

His sharp tone surprised me. "I'm just kidding."

"I know. But that's an awful thought." He pulled me closer and kissed me. When the kiss ended, his expression was gentler. "I just found you. It's depressing to think of things going back to the way they were."

I agreed. Maybe we hadn't been together long, but I was already rather hooked on this thing we had. He satisfied parts of me I hadn't even realized needed satisfying. I was emotionally and physically fulfilled. I couldn't remember a time in my life when that had been true before.

"I can do dinner Wednesday night," I said tentatively.

He didn't respond immediately, but then he said, "I'll call my mom tomorrow and set it up."

"Sounds good." *Sounds terrifying.*

"Sorry I snapped at you."

I laughed. "It's okay. It was kind of a dick thing to say to you; I'd rather die than meet your family?" I winced.

"So we can both be jerks." He grinned. "Yet another thing we share in common."

"It's uncanny how well suited we are." I smirked.

"Yeah." He sighed and went back to caressing my back.

****

When I got home from work the next day, Rafe was already there. Usually he came in way later than me, but tonight he sat on the couch with a glass of wine. The fact he had a drink was yet another thing that was different. Rafe wasn't a big drinker during the week. Seeing him, I immediately thought the worst. Had my test results come back and I really was dying or something?

"Hey," I said softly, as I approached him. "You're home way early."

His expression was odd. "Yeah. I am." He set his wine down and continued to stare at me.

I gave a nervous laugh. "Did the tests come back?"

"Yes."

I felt uneasy, and my legs were weak. I sat across from him, trying not to panic. "Is it bad?"

He pulled his dark brows tight. "Depends on your point of view."

What the heck does that mean?

"I don't understand." I swallowed hard.

"I don't quite know how to tell you what I need to tell you."

I pressed a hand to my thudding chest. "Jesus, Rafe. You're scaring the hell out of me."

His expression softened slightly. "Sorry. You're not dying."

Relief washed through me, and I closed my eyes. "God. You had me worried." I opened my eyes again. "You looked so grim when I came in."

"Sorry." He pressed his lips tight, and then said softly, "You don't have a disease or a virus."

I frowned. "Okay."

"You're not actually sick."

"But... how is that possible?" I touched my stomach, feeling puzzled. At the beginning of my shift today, I'd again spent half the morning in the store bathroom. Something was definitely wrong with me.

He raked a hand through his hair and said. "Against all odds..." He wrinkled his brow, looking perplexed. "Somehow... I don't understand how... but somehow... you're... pregnant."

Shock radiated through me and I simply stared at him wordlessly.

I'm pregnant?

"But... but..." That was the most I could say since my thoughts were a jumbled mess.

"I know. It's insane."

"I don't understand."

"Trust me, nor do I." He stood, and began to pace back and forth, looking irritable. "I'd have bet my life you couldn't conceive. I still can't believe it's possible. Your male ovaries were completely shielded by the omega pouch. There should be zero chance of sperm ever getting close enough to get you pregnant."

"You said my chances of getting pregnant were a bazillion to one."

"I'm aware of that. Obviously, I was wrong."

"But you're an expert. You're *the* expert."

"Don't you think I know that?" he snapped.

"I just can't believe it." I stared down at my clasped hands, feeling bewildered. I was too astonished to even accept that what he'd told me was the most amazing news in the world.

"This is a nightmare for me professionally. Now every omega I've ever told couldn't have kids will want a second opinion. Everyone will second guess my word."

"Not everyone. I mean, if you told them they couldn't have kids, then I'm sure most of them truly couldn't. Surely if they could, you'd have heard about it because they'd have gotten pregnant."

Like me. My God. I'm pregnant. I'm pregnant!

He huffed. "I can only pray this is some horrible fluke. This is professionally embarrassing for me." His callous, self-centered tone finally got to me.

I narrowed my eyes. "I have to say, your obtuse attitude right now is pretty fucked up. All you seem to care about is your reputation."

He flicked his emotionless glance to mine. "Well..."

"Maybe this is awkward for you, but for me it's the best thing in the world that you could have told me. If you actually cared about me, like you said you did, you'd know that." I touched my stomach. "I'm finally pregnant. That's what I've wanted more than anything in the world."

His face tensed. "Yes. Of course. I'm... I'm happy for you."

"You don't seem happy. You seem furious."

"It's complicated for me. I get that this is what you wanted. And I think it's great you can finally have the kid you craved. But for me it's different."

He sounded so detached it made me angry. "It's your child. You do realize that, right?"

"We don't know that."

I felt sick at his chilled statement. "Rafe, I haven't been with anyone but you since I split from Carlos. And I broke up with him almost two months ago. Plus Carlos hadn't had sex with me two months before that. He was too busy screwing his new omega behind my back."

His expression flickered. "We'll do a blood test to be sure."

I didn't know what to say. He'd just given me the most amazing news. By all rights, I should have been jumping with joy right at that moment. But instead, I was sick to my stomach at how selfish he was being. I felt like yelling at him, and telling him what an asshole he was, but I didn't want to get into a huge fight. That wouldn't solve anything.

Instead of letting him have it, I sucked in a deep breath. "There's no need to be so worried about your damn reputation. I'm sure you're safe. Only a very few people know you told me I was barren. None of your other patients will ever know your diagnosis of me was wrong."

He nodded slowly. "True." His expression was wary.

"After you told me I couldn't conceive, I didn't go on social media and announce it. I told my closest friends and my mom. That's it."

"Okay. Good."

Staring at his hard face, it was almost impossible to recognize him as the nurturing alpha he'd been the last few weeks. This person in front of me was cold and closed off emotionally. I felt disgusted looking at him. How could I have agreed to spend my life with an asshole like him? Had all his patience and kindness just been an act? Was he the kind of person who was only nice to you when it got him what he wanted?

I needed to get away from him before I said something unforgivable. I stood and moved to leave the room.

"Where are you going?" he asked sharply.

"To change out of my work clothes. Is that okay with you?"

He didn't respond, and I continued on my way to his bedroom. I grabbed some things from the dresser and went into the bathroom. I splashed my flushed face with cool water, and then touched my stomach. Staring at my reflection I looked scared. I felt terrified. Odds were Rafe was probably going to call it quits now. He'd made it more than clear he didn't like, or want kids. The only reason he'd chosen me as his omega was *because* he'd thought I couldn't get pregnant.

I leaned on the counter confused about what to feel. I was still so shocked at the idea I was pregnant, it hadn't really sunk in yet. I'd given up my place to move in with Rafe, and now I was in a mess. If he kicked me out, and he probably would, I'd have to find a new home and figure all of this out myself. It was terrifying to think about being pregnant without an alpha. For one thing, in our alpha omega society, it was frowned upon to be a single, pregnant omega. Unless your alpha died, or was abusive, when you had an alpha you were supposed to stick with them when pregnant.

The memory of Rafe's angry face made my stomach ache. I couldn't imagine sitting around all night with Rafe. Were we supposed to just go back to how it had been? That wasn't going to happen. Neither of us were the same now. I was hurt. I was angry with him. I certainly couldn't sit in the same room as him without saying something. And then what? We'd get in a huge fight and make everything even worse?

I left the bathroom and grabbed my cell and wallet. Then I tucked them into my back pocket and went back out into the living room. Thankfully, Rafe was in the kitchen, and I put my head down and headed for the front door. I had no idea where I was going, but I needed to get away from Rafe and his negative energy.

Beau Brown

Chapter Eight

"What did I tell you?" Stewart shook his head. "I knew he was an arrogant prick, and it would show itself sooner or later."

Polly gave Stewart an impatient glance. "I agree he was an asshole to you tonight, Peter, but all of this is a huge shock for him too."

"I know that," I grumbled. "But that doesn't excuse him making me feel like shit on what should be one of the happiest days of my life."

She rubbed my shoulder. "I know."

"Once and asshole always an asshole, that's what I say," Stewart finished his margarita, and signaled the bartender for another. "He has a lot of nerve making you feel like you've done something wrong, when he's the guy who knocked you up."

"He doesn't believe it's his." They both gasped in unison, and so I added, "I should say he still thinks there's a chance it could be Carlos' kid."

"Well, there is that slim chance. Best to know the truth up front." Polly sounded reasonable.

"Fuck him." Stewart scowled. "He should have hugged you and congratulated you, not made you feel bad."

I gave him a grateful glance. It felt nice to have someone a thousand percent on my side. I knew Polly was trying to be more balanced, but I was hurt. I was gutted. I just wanted to hear what a bastard Rafe was right now. I didn't want logic. I wanted people on my side telling me what a dick he was. I hadn't done anything wrong, and yet Rafe had made me feel like a fool.

Polly sighed and sipped her wine. She set her glass down and said, "He's probably going to feel like a heel for acting that way."

"Good," I muttered.

She laughed. "I know. He obviously was an ass to you. But you seemed like you really liked him only yesterday."

"I did. He was nice to me then. Today I saw that the real him, the asshole him that lurks just beneath the surface. Now I know that if things don't go his way, he turns back into that dick I met the first day."

"Amen." Stewart lifted his new drink.

"Stewart, stop. I'm trying to keep Peter calm. You're going to work him up again."

"Hey, I'm supporting my buddy." Stewart scowled.

"So am I. But getting him too angry won't solve anything."

Stewart rolled his eyes. "Whatever, Polly. You always know best."

She frowned. "I do not."

"You think you do," he grumbled.

"Come on you two. The last thing I need right now is you two at each other's throats." I gave them both a chiding look.

"Sorry." Stewart winced. "I just never liked the guy."

Polly sighed and picked up her wine. "This really sucks. I'm sorry, Peter."

I sipped my root beer, wishing like hell I could have a real drink. How could Rafe have been so cold to me? He'd really had me fooled. I'd thought we were getting closer and closer, and I'd started developing real feelings for him. Obviously, he'd felt differently. He'd never have been able to treat me the way he had tonight, if he really cared about me. I felt like such an idiot for even thinking he might actually fall for me eventually.

"So what are you going to do?" Polly asked. "You're welcome to crash on my couch."

"Thanks." I sighed. Polly's apartment was the size of a very large walk in closet. I was sure she knew staying at her place would never work longer than a couple of nights.

"You can stay with me too. I have a spare bedroom that I never use," Stewart offered.

"I might just have to take you up on that. At least until I can figure out my next move." I poked at the condensation on my glass. "This is so unfair. I finally get what I want and it explodes my whole world."

"Isn't that how life is sometimes? It never seems like you can have it all. You get pieces of things you want, and that's it." Stewart rested his chin on his palm.

"Well, I for one think it will all work out." Polly sounded falsely bright. "The most amazing part is you're pregnant. You're actually pregnant, Peter!" She leaned on me and kissed my cheek. "You just need to find a place to live, and we'll help you out with babysitting and stuff like that."

I swallowed hard, grateful for her sunny attitude, but still hugely worried. "The thing is, how will I work when I get later in the pregnancy? Without work I have no income. That isn't exactly how I wanted things."

"You can bring the baby to work with you. Keep it in the back, and no customers will be the wiser." Stewart winked at me.

"Yeah. Until the kid starts crying." I grimaced.

"It will be okay. We'll make it work," Stewart reassured me.

"We won't abandon you. Don't worry. We're in this with you, Peter." Polly gave me an encouraging smile.

"You can stay with me as long as you like." Stewart put his arm around my shoulder. "Seriously, I would love the company. It's lonely all alone in that big house."

"Yeah, but what if you meet someone?" I asked. "You're not going to want me and a baby hanging around."

"There are no real prospects on the horizon yet. Let's worry about that if it happens. For now, you need a safe place to crash, and I'm happy to offer that." Stewart sounded sincere.

"Okay. One step at a time." I nodded, rubbing my stomach.

"So are you going back there tonight?" Polly asked, a little line between her brows. "I'd hate for you two to get in some huge fight."

I sighed. "I don't know what to do. If I don't go back there, I won't know where I stand with Rafe."

Stewart bugged his eyes. "Dude, I think you know exactly where you stand with him. He doesn't want kids and you're pregnant. I'd say it's very cut and dried."

"No. I agree with Peter. They need to talk. If they're going to end things they need to officially have that conversation. It wouldn't be right for Peter to just abandon Rafe until they've figured this shit out."

"Seems pretty fucking figured out to me," muttered Stewart.

"I know I need to face him again." My voice wobbled. "The baby is his, I'm positive."

"Then he better pitch in financially and not be a jerk about it." Stewart scowled.

"I'm sure one of his top priorities will be to figure out if the kid is his, or not. He's no doubt praying it's Carlos' so he can completely wash his hands of me." I felt sick remembering how cold and distant Rafe had been tonight. It was hard to accept. I'd been so happy the last week, and it was demoralizing to realize Rafe wasn't the man I'd thought he was.

"Personally, I think it would serve him right if you don't go back to his place tonight. Stay with me. Cool off and you can go talk with him tomorrow." Stewart glanced at his watch as he spoke. "It's already eleven. You don't want to go back there and get into a big thing this late at night."

"True." I had to fight an odd urge to go back to Rafe. Even though he'd been a colossal dick to me tonight, my inner omega wanted to be near him. He'd claimed me, and I'd accepted. It wasn't going to be easy to change my instinctual desire to be with him. At least, it wasn't going to happen in one night. "God, I would kill for a drink right now."

Stewart grimaced. "You could probably have one and it wouldn't hurt the baby."

Polly shook her head. "No way you should chance that, Peter. Not when you've waited so long to get pregnant."

I stared longingly at Stewart's margarita. "Nah. I'll just stick it out with my root beer."

"Good." Polly stood. "I'm going to the restroom. Be back." She wandered away.

"So what are you going to do? Coming home with me tonight?" Peter studied me.

"I think I should. I'm too tired to have a rational conversation with Rafe, and I'm pretty hurt, so I might lash out." I met his sympathetic gaze. "You sure it's okay to stay with you?"

"I'm looking forward to it." He laughed. "I get a little tired of talking to myself."

I smiled. "I'll bet."

"I'm really happy for you," he said softly. "I know how much you've wanted this."

"Thanks."

I was distracted from our conversation when an alpha wandered up. The guy was tall, dark haired and drunk. He swayed back and forth while staring at Stewart with a pissy expression. "Don't I know you?" He looked annoyed.

Stewart glanced at the guy. "Uh… no. Sorry."

"I'm sure I know you."

Wrinkling his brow, Stewart said. "You've got the wrong person."

The alpha scowled. "Come on dude, just admit it. We talked on Grindr the other night for like an hour. It's me, Sexy69."

"I think you have me confused with someone else." Stewart sounded patient, but he shifted uneasily.

"No. I'm sure it's you." Sexy69 pointed an unsteady finger at Stewart. "You ghosted me the other night. Why'd you do that? We were having a good conversation."

Stewart responded, "Dude, I haven't been on that app in over a month."

Sexy69 wasn't listening. "I know your face." His gaze dropped to the tattoo of a wolf on Stewart's arm. "I even recognize that tat."

"It wasn't me, man. Maybe someone is using my photo or something." Stewart turned his back on the guy, probably hoping he'd take the hint.

But the guy was way too drunk to be reasonable. He grabbed Stewart's shoulder and tugged. "Don't turn your back on me. I know it's you."

Stewart stiffened and pushed the guys hand off. "You need to keep your paws to yourself."

"Oh really?" Sexy69 hissed. "You made a lot of sexual promises. What's to stop me from just insisting you follow through?"

I scowled at the guy. "Seriously? Me for one. You think I'm just gonna sit here and let you assault my friend?"

The guy turned his angry gaze on me. "Butt out."

"Uh, no. I don't think so." There were a couple of younger alphas at the bar watching, but no one said anything to help out. That wasn't too unusual. This older alpha was probably higher up in the hierarchy than them.

Polly returned, looking confused about what was happening. "Everything okay?" she asked.

"This guy is just drunk," I said sharply.

"Yeah, can't hold his liquor." Stewart snorted.

"You two are pretty cocky for omegas," grumbled the guy.

Stewart exhaled tiredly and swiveled his chair to face the guy. "I'm sorry you got catfished or whatever. But I'm not on Grindr. I'm not looking to hook up tonight either. You should go find someone else to spend tonight with."

As if he hadn't heard a word Stewart had said, Sexy69 sneered. "I'll buy you a drink, and you can suck me off out back. How's that?"

Polly gasped. "Gross."

Stewart curled his lip. "That's not gonna happen. I can buy my own drinks, thanks."

Sexy69 grabbed Stewart's arm roughly, and I stood with a growl. But the guy caught me off guard when he elbowed me, and I landed on my ass on the sawdust covered floor.

Polly let out a screech and covered her cheeks with her hands. "What are you doing?"

"Mind your own business," snapped Sexy69.

Just then an alpha who'd been sitting quietly nearby stood, and put his arm around Sexy69's neck. "Let him go, asshole," rumbled the alpha.

I scrambled to my feet, brushing the sawdust off my jeans. "Yeah, get the fuck away from my friend."

When the other alpha grabbed him, Sexy69 immediately released his grip on Stewart, and his eyes were wide. "Fine. Fine. I didn't know he was with you, Lex."

"Go sober up somewhere else," Lex snarled. "You give alpha's a bad name."

"I'm going. I'm going." Sexy69 stumbled away, giving a nervous glance back toward us as he left the bar.

"Thanks," I said breathlessly, still trying to swat the sawdust from my pant legs.

"No problem." Lex raked a hand through his blond hair and glanced toward Stewart. "You okay?"

Nodding, Stewart said, "I'm fine." His cheeks were flushed, but he seemed unharmed.

I vaguely recognized Lex. "Wait... I think I know you."

Lex grimaced, looking a little embarrassed.

"You've come in to the shop where we work a few times, right?" I laughed and nudged Stewart's arm. "This is flannel shirt guy."

"Oh, yeah," Stewart said, studying Lex.

"What?" Polly laughed, giving Lex a curious look.

Lex grimaced. "Flannel shirt guy? You have a name for me?"

Stewart nodded, his expression amused. "Yeah. We have names for a lot of our regulars."

"Do I really buy that many flannel shirts?" Lex laughed gruffly.

Screwing his face up, Stewart said, "Well, you've bought three in the last month; the blue one with the red stripe, then the red one with the blue stripe, oh and the yellow one. I really liked that one. It looked great on you."

Lex's cheeks were pink. "They're mighty comfy."

Stewart grinned. "Apparently."

I sat down and gestured to an empty bar stool near Stewart. "Can we buy you a drink, Lex?"

Stewart nodded. "Yeah. It's the least we can do."

"Nah." Lex moved to grab his beer off his table, and he returned to sit next to Stewart. "I have a drink. But thanks."

"I really appreciate you chasing that guy off." Stewart sighed. "He's wrong. I really haven't been on Grindr in ages."

"I believe you," Lex said quietly.

Watching the two of them, I got the feeling they were into each other. Their knees were touching and neither of them made any move to pull their leg away. Lex seemed like a nice guy. Sexy too. I also had to respect that he'd been the only person in the bar willing to step in. Stewart had said he was interested in meeting a good alpha and settling down. Who knew, maybe Lex was someone he'd really connect with. Lex had already proved he had a protective streak by chasing off that other alpha.

A nudge of melancholy hit me at the memory of how I'd foolishly thought I'd found my alpha too. God, how wrong I'd been. Rafe had treated me, and my pregnancy, like nothing more than a burden tonight. What was it about me that seemed to attract the wrong type of alphas?

I stood, and Stewart looked over. "I think I might take off. I'm beat."

"Oh, yeah, sure."

Polly rose as well. "Me too." She tossed money on the counter and pushed it toward the bartender. "Keep the change."

"Thanks." The guy smiled.

"Can't thank you enough for standing up for us, Lex." My voice was gruff as I met his gaze.

"My pleasure." Lex gave Stewart a little glance under his lashes.

Stewart pulled his keys from his pocket and he slid one off. "Here's my spare."

I took the key, feeling awkward doing that in front of Lex. But he didn't ask any questions, and I didn't volunteer an explanation. We said our goodbyes, and Polly and I walked to the parking lot.

When we reached our cars, she gave me a long hug. "Are you going to be okay?"

"Yeah." My eyes stung at the concern in her voice. "I've been hurt before." I gave a raspy laugh. "I sure can pick 'em, eh?"

"Aww, honey. I'm so sorry Rafe turned out to be an asshole."

"Me too." I swallowed against the lump in my throat and unlocked my car.

Her eyes glittered with concern in the street lights. "Promise me you'll call me tomorrow?"

"Sure." I smiled weakly. "Night."

"Night, Peter."

I got in my car and started the engine, giving her a fake smile. I didn't want her to worry about me. Yes, I was crushed. I almost hadn't realized, until Rafe turned on me, just how much I was falling for him. He'd done a great job of reeling me in and giving me the affection and attention I'd always wanted from an alpha. It was going to be tough to just turn off my feelings now. But I'd have to. Just like I'd done with Carlos when he'd shown his true colors too.

I let myself into Stewart's house and headed to the guest room. I'd crashed with him a few times when I'd had too many drinks. But tonight felt depressing. I was basically hiding from Rafe. I needed space so I could think clearly about what to do next.

I stripped off my clothes and, wearing just my underwear, I crawled into the sheets. I curled into a ball and hugged my stomach. There was a life inside me, growing slowly each day. I needed to think about that, instead of how hard it was to breathe because I was so depressed. This little baby relied on me for everything at this stage. I wouldn't let it down either. I'd protect my unborn child with everything I had in me. If that meant living with Stewart until I was able to afford a place on my own, then so be it.

What if Stewart finds an alpha?

My gut clenched with nerves. I wanted the best for my friend. Now that he'd decided he was ready to find an alpha, I'd never get in the way of that. But I wasn't going to worry about it just yet.

Tomorrow I'd buy prenatal vitamins and start eating healthy. At least now I knew why I'd been so sick. It was a relief to know that it wasn't anything bad. Life altering, yes, but in a wonderful way.

In spite of my strange predicament, a smile spread across my tense face, as I stroked my belly. There was a life inside me and I hadn't even known it. Who was it? What was it? Girl or boy? I didn't care which gender, so long as it was healthy. What would its personality be like? Even if Rafe didn't want to admit it, I knew the baby was his. Would the child take after him? Would it be an omega or an alpha? My heart ached as Rafe's face swam before my blurry eyes. God, I'd loved touching him and being in his arms. Would I ever find that again? I'd only been officially with him two weeks, and yet they'd been the best two weeks of my life.

How could the loving alpha I'd enjoyed for weeks, be the same one who'd stared down his nose at me today? I was still shaken remembering how unfeeling he'd been. In that moment, nothing had mattered to him except his fucking reputation. That hurt. That knowledge hurt so bad I felt lost. Adrift. Abandoned. Yeah, maybe I'd run out on him tonight, but in all honesty, he'd left me first; the minute he'd discovered I was pregnant.

I needed to stop thinking about his warm golden eyes, his scent, and the sound of his husky voice. I'd now have to let go all those feelings that had taken root the last month. Rafe wasn't who I'd thought he was, and I just needed to accept that and move on.

Beau Brown

Chapter Nine

The next morning I woke to the sound of raised voices. I frowned, and pulled on my jeans, then I opened the bedroom door and listened. My stomach somersaulted when I recognized Rafe's voice. My first instinct was to slam the door closed and hide under the bed. But I couldn't leave poor Stewart to fight my battle for me. And from the sound of their angry voices, there was definitely an altercation of some sort happening.

I hurried down the hallway toward the voices. I found Stewart and Rafe in the foyer by the front door. Stewart had on his robe, and his hair stood up as if he'd just crawled out of bed. His shoulders were bunched as he blocked Rafe's path, and the alpha didn't look any too happy about Stewart being in his way. Rafe was at least three inches taller, and twenty pounds heavier than my friend, and I had little doubt he could toss Stewart aside if he really wanted. But I had to respect how bravely Stewart held his ground.

"What's going on?" I stood behind Stewart and put my hand on his shoulder as a sign of solidarity.

Rafe looked past Stewart, his mouth a grim line. "Why didn't you come home last night?"

"You know why."

Stewart continued to block Rafe, but he glanced at me over his shoulder. "He wants to come in and talk to you. I... I wasn't sure you wanted that."

"He's my omega," growled Rafe. "I have every right to talk to him."

"I don't want you as my alpha anymore," I snapped, feeling kind of sick at the look of shock that swam across Rafe's face.

"Since when?" he demanded, masking his hurt expression.

"Since you turned back into the asshole I suspected you were from the beginning."

He pressed his lips tight and dropped his gaze to Stewart. "Look, I'm sure you mean well, but I need to talk to Peter. *Privately*."

I heard Stewart swallow. He shifted uneasily and looked at me again. "What do you want to do?"

I sighed. I didn't really want to talk to Rafe. I was afraid he'd only say more mean things that might depress me even further. But I knew I probably should let him speak, if only so that he'd then go away and leave us alone. I didn't want Stewart getting hurt trying to protect me.

"I'll talk to him," I said softly.

A gleam of satisfaction appeared in Rafe's amber eyes.

I addressed my alpha. "Only because I want you to leave, and I assume that's the only way to get what I want." I kept my voice cool, and my gaze hard.

Rafe narrowed his eyes, but he didn't speak.

Stewart moved back and gave me a searching look. "Are you sure? I don't want him to bully you."

"Bully him?" Rafe sounded insulted. "Why would I do that?"

Stewart scowled. "Because you're an alpha and you think you should always get your way."

Rafe sniffed. "That's not true."

"Says the alpha trying to barge his way into my house." Stewart chuffed.

"Are you going to leave us in private or not?" Rafe raised one dark brow.

"It's okay." I touched my friends shoulder. "We can go out front on the porch."

"All right." Stewart looked less than thrilled. "But if you need me, just yell."

"I will." I watched Stewart retreat to the kitchen, and then I met Rafe's gaze. "After you." I gestured toward the door.

He turned and exited the house, and I followed, closing the door behind me. My pulse skittered crazily because he looked so handsome, and he smelled deliciously familiar. A part of me just wanted him to take me in his arms and tell me it had all been a horrible mistake.

I crossed my arms as he faced me. "I'm not sure we have anything to talk about."

His jaw hardened. "Bullshit."

"What is there to say, Rafe? You made your position pretty fucking clear last night."

"Look, I was in shock."

"I'm sure you were. But that doesn't excuse how heartless you were." My voice wobbled with emotion. "I barely recognized you."

He pushed a shaky hand through his dark hair, scowling. "That's no excuse for you to just run off without a word. Didn't it occur to you I might be worried? Why the hell didn't you at least text me so I knew you were alive?"

"I didn't think what happened to me, or the baby, was really very important to you. You made it obvious you didn't give a shit about me anymore."

"That... that isn't true."

"I guess now it's my turn to say bullshit."

He hung his head. "Jesus, Peter, I know I fucked up." His voice was hoarse.

I was shocked at his raw emotion. "What?"

He met my gaze, his face red and his eyes full of shame. "I slipped back into my old ways, and all I could think about was my reputation. I'm sick that I made you feel awful about being pregnant. I know you needed that, and prayed for that, and I just crapped all over your happy moment."

It was hard to believe I was hearing him right. "Why would you suddenly be nice again?"

He scowled. "Because I am nice." He winced. "Usually."

"You mean to tell me you now want this baby?" I gave him a suspicious stare.

He flinched. "Well, not exactly. I mean, I can't just suddenly feel elated that you're pregnant, when I've told you I don't want kids. I don't want to lie to you."

My stomach clenched with disappointment. "Then why are you here?"

"Because I want you to come home."

I had no idea what to feel when those words left his mouth. "You didn't even believe me when I told you this was your baby," I said coolly.

He winced again. "God. I know. But to be honest, there is a chance the kid is Carlos'. That's just a fact."

"Fuck you," I growled, and I turned to go back inside.

He moved swiftly, and he grabbed my arm. "No. Wait! Peter, please don't go inside."

The feel of his fingers on my skin made my knees weak. I hated myself for wanting to give into him. But my desire to please him was strong, as the omega in me responded to his touch. I lifted my chin and hoped I looked unaffected by his hand on me. "This baby is yours. I haven't slept with Carlos in four months, and you've fucked me bareback since we met. Stop insulting my intelligence by pretending this baby might not be yours."

He held up his hand. "Okay. I agree the baby is probably mine."

I eyed him warily. "You really believe that?"

He nodded. "Odds are, it's mine."

At least he'd finally admitted that.

He glanced at his fingers wrapped around my wrist and he let go. "Either way... I want you back."

Pleasure mixed with uncertainty at his heartfelt announcement. "That's sudden."

"I never said I didn't want *you*." His comment hung awkwardly in the air.

I winced. "Yeah, well, the baby and I are a package deal."

"I know that."

"I don't understand why you'd want me back. I'm pregnant. You don't want kids. You should go find yourself some other omega. But be sure they're actually barren this time, before you get their hopes up." My voice quivered, and I hardened my jaw. I didn't want him seeing how much he'd hurt me.

He leaned against the wooden railing of the porch and stared off across the yard. We stood in silence for a few moments, and then he spoke quietly. "My initial plan was just you and I. We both know that, so there's no point in pretending otherwise." He cleared his throat. "You think I haven't changed or that I don't really care. That's not true. The old me would have let you run last night, and the old me would have been happy you were gone. I didn't want kids, and since you'd left me, problem solved."

I scowled at him, not sure what his point was.

"But spending this last month with you has done something to me. Although, if I'm being frank, there are times I wished I'd never met you."

"If this is you trying to woo me, you're not very good at it."

He scrunched his features. "I just want you to really see me clearly. I'm a selfish man, I know that. I like things the way I like them, and I haven't had any trouble finding people willing to give me what I want." He turned his head to look at me. "Until I met you."

"But I was willing to give you what you wanted."

"No. You couldn't have what you wanted, and by default that gave me what I wanted; no kids." He grimaced. "But now that you have a choice, you're standing up for what you need. I have to respect that, even though it interferes with my own selfish desires."

"Why did you wish you'd never met me?" I asked breathlessly.

He sighed. "Because I felt myself growing too attached." He bit his bottom lip. "You were on my mind too much. It made me uneasy. It made me feel dependent on you. Weak even. That's not how I am usually. I'm not generally terribly affectionate or needy. But with you... I don't recognize myself."

I had to admit he did look confused.

He cleared his throat. "I don't want to be clingy or needy. I don't want to miss you when you're gone. All those things make me feel exposed and vulnerable. That's not something alphas like. I much prefer to be in control. I prefer to have the omega feeling all those things, not me."

"I do feel those things too." Those six words escaped before I could stop them. My face warmed when he pinned his gaze on me.

"Really?"

"You must know I do." My voice was soft, and I avoided looking at him. "Part of why I'm so hurt is because I… I do have feelings for you. And you made it obvious last night that you didn't want me anymore… if I was pregnant."

"Well… I didn't mean that. I was just being a self-pitying asshole."

"But that must be how you feel deep down. Yeah, maybe it sucked to hear you say all that shit, but the bottom line is, that's how you felt or you wouldn't have said it."

"But I wasn't even really dealing with your pregnancy. It wasn't real to me last night. All I was thinking was people would doubt me and it could hurt my rep. After you left, I had time to think about how all of this was affecting *you*. And I remembered--" He swallowed hard. "I remembered your face… and I wanted to crawl under a rock."

I shrugged, a lump in my throat making speech difficult.

"I wish I could turn back time. I wish I could do it over again and do it right this time." He rubbed his face roughly and then dropped his hands limply at his side. "I should have brought home a bottle of champagne and some flowers. I should have kissed you and held you, and told you how happy I was that you'd finally got what you wanted most." His eyes were red rimmed as he continued. "But I didn't. I can't bear to think that I've fucked everything up so bad I don't get to have you. That's not okay, Peter. That's just not fucking okay with me."

It was impossible not to feel moved by his passionate speech. He sounded sincere, and his face was flushed with raw emotion. When he took a step toward me, I didn't flinch away. And when he slid his arms around me, I let him. In fact, I leaned into him, and buried my face in his chest, scared and confused, but craving his touch.

"Come home," he whispered. "I want you back where you belong. We'll figure the rest out."

I sniffed, my eyes stinging. It felt amazing to hear him say he still wanted me. But the child I carried had to be my priority. "I'm having this baby."

"God, I know that, Peter. Do you really think I'd ask you to get rid of it?" He sounded hurt, and he pulled back to search my face. "I'd never do that to you. I know this child is all you've ever wanted."

I winced. "Well, I wanted an alpha too. Not just the baby. I wanted the whole thing."

His amber eyes warmed with hope. "You can have that. We can have a family. That's what you really want, right? A family?"

I nodded slowly. "Yes."

"Well…" He captured his lower lip between his teeth. "That doesn't seem so bad anymore. Not if… not if it's with you."

I scanned his face, searching for any hint of doubt. "Don't say that shit to me if it's not real."

"It is real." His tone was bemused. "Somewhere along the way I've fallen for you." He looked almost scared as those words left his lips. "That wasn't the plan. Not at all. But… I can't help it." He rubbed his chest. "You're in here so deep I can't get you out even if I wanted to."

Excitement and disbelief wrestled in my heart. "You think you're ready to be a dad?"

He blanched a little. "I think so… I'd better be." He gave a weak laugh. "You'll be patient with me, right? This probably won't come naturally to me. You'll help me?"

"It'll be the blind leading the blind, but yeah, I'll do anything I can to make it easier on you." Was this actually happening? Was Rafe holding me and telling me he wanted me? That he wanted to be a family with me? I almost couldn't comprehend that idea.

He lowered his head and kissed me. The feel of his warm lips on mine coaxed a whimper from me and I clung to him. If this was all real, I'd found my alpha. I'd found my family. If this was real, I'd found my happiness.

Beau Brown

Chapter Ten

"Oh, shit." I scrambled to try and right the spilled can of paint, but I tripped over the pole attached to the roller, and ended up on my rear end. I grabbed the paint can and tipped it upright with an impatient sigh. I next pulled off an arm's length of paper towels and dabbed at the mess. "God, I swear I really have painted before. I'm usually much more skilled."

"You know... I can handle this on my own." Rafe's amused voice came from above. He was on a ladder trying to get the highest corners of the room.

I laughed as I got to my feet. "Be quiet. I only fell because I didn't want the paint to ruin your expensive carpet."

"That's why we have a canvas tarp over it." He stifled a laugh. "Nice dive though. I give it an eight."

"Ha. Ha." I rolled my eyes and picked up my roller. I dipped it in the yellow pigment and returned to painting the wall. "I didn't expect you to spend your day off doing this. Just so you know."

He stopped painting and glanced down at me. "Why wouldn't I help?"

I shrugged and kept painting.

"Still think I only have one foot in?"

Sometimes.

"Of course not," I responded brightly. I focused on a stubborn patch where the paint didn't want to fill in the dips in the stucco. I wanted to believe Rafe was all in, but he'd been so adamant about not wanting kids initially, it was hard to accept his swift change of heart.

He huffed and slowly made his way down the ladder. He peeled off his gloves and tossed them onto the canvas. Then he moved closer to me, wearing a very serious expression. "You can talk to me about anything. If you're feeling insecure, I want you to talk to me. Don't pretend everything is fine if it isn't."

My stomach swirled with excitement as he neared, the way it always did when he came close. He just did something to me physically that no other alpha had. From the start, our sexual connection had been there, but it was definitely turning into much more. Ever since we'd had our little fight over my pregnancy, I'd begun to truly fall for him. When he'd chased after me, and brought me back to his home, I'd started to believe that maybe he loved me. He'd never actually said those words to me, but I certainly felt loved. He treated me as if I was the most important person in his life. I'd never had that before from an alpha, and I prayed it was true.

He stopped in front of me, and he placed his hand on my slightly bulged belly. The warmth of his palm sank into me, and I sighed, immediately comforted by my alpha's touch. "This is our baby, Peter. Ours." His voice was husky.

I nodded, feeling emotional.

"I won't pretend that I'm not nervous to meet this little person. I mean, what if it doesn't like me or something?" He frowned, pulling his brows together.

I smiled, my heart squeezing. "He or she will like you."

"I'll probably be a strict parent." He sighed. "It's my nature. Nobody likes the dad who enforces a curfew, so the baby will like you better."

"This child will like us both and I'm not exactly a push over."

"You have a gentleness about you that comes naturally to an omega." His voice was warm. "You'll be an incredible father."

"I hope so. It would suck if I was horrible at being a dad after wanting this for so long."

"No way." He kissed me softly.

I slipped my arms around his waist and opened my mouth hungrily. He pushed his tongue inside, deepening the kiss. His hands ran down the small of my back, to cup my ass. His crotch was raised and firm and I knew he wanted me. We couldn't seem to keep our hands off of each other. I wasn't sure if it was hormones that had me ready to jump his bones at every opportunity, or because I felt so bonded to him.

He groaned and slowly unzipped my jeans. "I want to fuck you." He sounded breathless as he stroked my cock through the thin cotton of my underwear.

I nodded and glanced over at the futon against the far wall. I grabbed his hand and led him over to the bed, and together we unfolded the thin mattress. Then we both got down on the futon, and I lay on top of him with a flirtatious smile.

"I want to be on top today," I said, meeting his amorous gaze.

He blinked at me, looking uneasy. "Really?"

I smiled. "You can still fuck me, but I want to be on top."

He let out a shaky breath. "Oh, okay."

Something about his nervous reaction made me pause. "Do you never bottom?" We'd never discussed that stuff. It was common for the omegas to be the bottom, but I'd topped Carlos a few times. Admittedly, most alphas didn't like giving up that control though.

"No." He licked his lips. "But... but I would for you."

Surprise washed through me, and I leaned down and kissed him again, sighing against his lips. When I lifted my head, I said, "That means a lot to me."

His eyes sparked with need. "I just want you happy."

"I am happy."

"Okay. Me too."

I grinned. "You just want to get to the sex part, huh?"

"Please."

I twisted my lips and unzipped his pants, holding his gaze. "Maybe one day I'll take you up on your offer. But right now? I just want you inside me."

He hissed as I slid my hand into the flap of his pants and cupped his swollen dick. "You drive me nuts." He pressed against my palm, his lips parted and his eyes heated. "I can't wait for you to slide down on me."

"We should lose the pants."

"Agreed." His pulse beat swiftly in the base of his throat as he wiggled out of his pants and underwear. His cock was stiff and seeping as it bobbed against his flat stomach. As he'd stripped off his jeans, I'd managed to get out of mine as well. I moved to straddle his thighs, feeling hungry for him. He rested his hands on my hips, his eyes glittering salaciously as a little whimper escaped his lips.

"You want this ass?" I smirked, smoothing my hands up his rigid cock. The head seeped, and I used that pre-cum to make his thick length slick. I worked his dick, squeezing the firm flesh and stroking him slowly. "Because I want this beautiful cock in me."

His fingers dug into my skin and he arched his back. "I need to fuck you now."

"Patience, Grasshopper." I licked my lips, fighting the urge to give him what he wanted, and immediately slip down on his cock. "I want you so turned on you come the second you're inside me."

"No. I want it to last. I want to fuck you long and hard and then fill your ass."

I gave him a smug look as I squeezed and jerked his cock more insistently. "We'll do it my way or we don't do it at all, alpha."

He panted and nodded, his eyes bright with need. "Okay. Okay. Just please hurry."

He moaned and pulsed his hips as I worked his cock, running my hands up and down his thick length. "You still gonna want to fuck me when my belly is big?" I swiped my thumb over the wide head, teasing the slit.

"Yeah." His eyes glittered with lust. "I want to fill you with more babies too."

My pulse spiked. "Is that right?"

"I'll keep you fat and pregnant with my children." He moaned and slipped his hands under my ass, squeezing the tender flesh. His fingers found their way to my hole, and I hissed as he rubbed the tips of his fingers over my entrance.

My lust ramped as he pushed against my hole. "I love it when you touch me," I whispered.

"Yeah?" His voice was hoarse.

"I need you." I lifted myself and hovered over his cock.

He grabbed his dick and held it straight, his gaze locked with mine. "Fuck yourself on me, Peter. Use me."

My heart pounded as I lowered myself, and the head of his cock pushed against my hole. The pressure and anticipation had me light headed with need. "Oh, god," I whimpered as I sank down on his shaft. I shuddered as he entered me, the wide head of his dick popping past my ring of muscle. "Oh, fuck."

He groaned and flexed his hips, seating himself deeper inside me. His fingers dug into my thighs, perspiration breaking out on his forehead. "So good," he moaned, thrusting upward.

I threw my head back and rode his cock, up and down, up and down, the friction making my nipples and cock hard. I tensed my muscles, needing him so much it terrified me. I'd never craved anyone like I did him. When he was inside me, I felt complete, loved, wanted. He never held back when we fucked. I could feel his need and vulnerability so tangibly. He'd probably have hated the idea I could see inside him that way, but I could.

My leg muscles burned as I fucked myself on his shaft, seeking that release I needed so bad. I opened my eyes and met his fervent gaze, his lips were parted and his desire written so clearly on his beautiful face. "Mine," he growled, thrusting harder. "Only, mine."

"Yeah," I panted, my eyes rolling up into my head because it felt so good. "Just you. Just you."

"Look at me," he whispered hoarsely.

My eyes were blurry as I obeyed, meeting his heated gaze.

"I love you, Peter. I love you." His voice shook.

Inexplicable joy radiated through me as those words left his lips. "Me too. I love you too."

He smiled and then groaned, arching his back, he came hard, filling me with his cum. He bucked his hips as I began jerking myself roughly.

I was right there; hovering on a cliff of delicious pleasure, my orgasm quivering on the verge of exploding. And then my muscles clenched involuntarily and released, catapulting me into ecstasy. Cum flowed over my hands as I squeezed and tugged through my climax. "Oh, fuck, *fuck*." I shuddered and twitched because it felt so good it was almost unbearable.

"Yeah, come for me." He watched me, his expression still clouded with lust. He rolled his hips and moaned, still obviously enjoying the moment.

My muscles were weak as my orgasm slowly faded like the morning tide. I slumped and struggled to catch my breath. "God damn." I gave a feeble laugh.

His expression was serious as he watched me, stroking his hands over my thighs. He looked like he wanted to say something, but he didn't. He just continued to caress my skin.

I pulled off of him and collapsed beside him. He turned, and we embraced, neither of us seeming to care that my abs were covered in cum. We kissed, long, gentle kisses that soothed me. He tightened his grip on me. "I meant what I said," he whispered.

"I did too." My mouth was dry as I spoke. "It meant everything to hear you say you loved me."

"I couldn't hold it in anymore."

"Why would you need to?"

He shrugged one shoulder. "Sometimes it's hard to admit that I've fallen in love. This wasn't how I pictured my future. There was no pregnant omega in my fantasies." He gave a gruff laugh. "Now I can't see my destiny without you in it; you and our child. It's very weird. How could my perspective change so completely and so quickly?"

"I don't know. I've always wanted this." I grimaced. "But I didn't think I'd get it." I glanced up at him, feeling emotionally exposed. "But from the moment I met you... something happened inside me."

"Me too." He pushed the hair off my forehead, his expression warm. "When I saw you in the bar that night, I had to connect with you. I needed you to forgive me. I knew you were mad at me, but I couldn't let it lie."

"Well, I'm glad. Because this wouldn't be happening if you'd let your pride guide you."

"True enough."

I glanced down at my sticky belly. "I'm a mess."

He grinned. "Yeah."

"A happy mess."

"Oh, well. With a kid on the way, I'd better get used to messes."

"And noise. You'll have to get used to lots of noise too."

He wrinkled his brow. "I have my omega and a kid on the way. If someone had told me this would be my life two months ago, I'd have laughed them out of the room."

"Me too. Life's full of surprises."

"Yeah, and as a doctor, I'm not usually fond of surprises."

"I get that."

He touched my cheek. "I'm beginning to think unexpected things are the best part of life. All of these twists and turns lately have brought me to you, and our child."

"Very true." I snuggled closer to him. "I'm so glad I didn't go to the fertility specialist my insurance covered. None of this would have happened."

"That's scary to think that something as simple as you not showing up at my office would have changed the course of my life so much." He tightened his hold. "I hate the very idea of that."

"You sure you don't just sometimes want your perfect life back?"

"What?" He scowled. "Perfect? What was perfect about it? I was self-centered and alone. My home life was as sterile as my work life. I thought emotional attachments interfered with happiness, when in fact, they create all the good stuff."

"I agree. Yes, emotions can be complicated and messy, but they're what it's all about."

"Absolutely. Bring on the mess." He laughed softly.

I grimaced. "Just remember you said that, when you're covered in pureed carrots, and changing dirty diapers."

"Would it be odd for me to wear a hazmat suit around the baby?"

I grinned. "Probably."

"Okay, fine. Because I love you, I'll just let the little monster toss peas at me and not complain."

I sighed contentedly. "When you say things like that, I know you really do love me."

He brushed his lips over my hair. "With all my heart, Peter."

Beau Brown

Chapter Eleven

"You've stalled and stalled but I finally get to meet you." Mrs. Hexton smiled warmly as she threw open the door. "I've been nagging my son for three months to drag you over here."

"Sorry. I wasn't feeling that great the first trimester." I grimaced.

She surprised me with a hug, and when she let go she said, "Well, you're here now. That's all that matters." She stepped aside, and Rafe ushered me into the big house.

While Rafe embraced his mom, I examined the area. The floors of the vestibule were marble, and an enormous crystal chandelier hung over our heads. I definitely felt intimidated by the obvious elegance and wealth that surrounded me; and this was just the foyer. The press of Rafe's hand on the small of my back helped calm me a bit, and when we followed his mother into a big room off the entrance, there were three people waiting with big grins on their faces.

Rafe nudged me into the room when I started to hesitate. "Come on, meet the family."

I laughed awkwardly, locking eyes with a younger version of Rafe.

"I'm the boyish, better looking Hexton." Jaden held out his hand, his smile genuine.

"Keep telling yourself that." Rafe didn't sound truly miffed, and his easygoing smile proved he wasn't.

There was a girl about fourteen who marched up and stuck her hand out. "I'm Stephany, with a 'Y'."

"I didn't know that was a thing." I shook her hand.

"It is. Mostly because there was a mistake on my birth certificate, but I like it. Makes me unique." She shrugged, brushing her blonde and pink streaked hair off her shoulders.

"That's not the only thing that makes you... unique." Mrs. Hexton laughed.

Mr. Hexton also approached. "I'm Rafe's dad."

"How do you do, Mr. Hexton?" I took his firm grip.

"Please, call me Tom."

I nodded, feeling a little conspicuous with all eyes trained on me. I patted my plump belly with a nervous laugh. I was showing, and obviously pregnant to anyone who bothered to really look, but I didn't have a huge stomach yet. "I'd introduce you to the baby, but we don't know whether it's a girl or a boy."

"Oh, so long as it's healthy," Mrs. Hexton said cheerfully. "Forgive our excitement, but this is our first grand-baby."

"I understand. I don't know how much Rafe has told you, but it's my first baby too."

Mrs. Hexton gave her son a smirk. "He hasn't told us much. We could have used some info too because, believe me, when Rafe said he'd chosen an omega and that he'd gotten the omega pregnant as well, we were all in shock."

"I'm sure." I shifted uneasily, my feet were swollen, and I was tired as usual.

Rafe must have noticed I looked uncomfortable. "Why don't we sit and visit?" He had me sit on the sofa, and he joined me.

"Of course. Sorry, I'm just so busy staring at poor Peter." She laughed and sat across from us.

"How are you feeling?" Tom asked. "Is the morning sickness all gone now?"

"Pretty much." I winced. "I still can't stand the smell of parsley for some reason, but other than that, I'm doing better."

"My best friend's mother got pregnant, and she barfed the whole way through the pregnancy," Stephany announced. "Anytime she picked us up for school she always looked a little green."

Everyone but me laughed. I felt too much sympathy for the poor woman.

"So how did you two meet?" Mrs. Hexton asked, crossing her hands in her lap.

I met Rafe's gaze, and I laughed. "We didn't start off that great to be honest."

Rafe smirked. "I still think it was love at first sight though."

I raised my brows.

Lust maybe.

"Mom just about fainted when Rafe told us he'd picked an omega." Stephany widened her eyes as she stared at her older brother. "He was adamant he didn't want to ever have kids or settle down. Then *poof*, he's done both."

Mrs. Hexton shrugged. "Well, it was a shock, but a happy shock. I'm so glad Rafe met someone who changed his mind."

I felt a little more relaxed because everyone was so welcoming. I leaned back against the couch. "I didn't think I could have kids. Lots of doctors told me I couldn't. But I went to Rafe because he's the leading expert in the area, and I wanted to be absolutely sure. He also said I'd never get pregnant."

Rafe scrunched his face with distaste. "I didn't just tell him that though. I was a complete jerk."

Mrs. Hexton frowned. "Really?"

I laughed gruffly. "He told me I had a better chance of being hit by a meteor."

They all three gasped, and Rafe winced.

I added quickly, "He's since apologized over and over again."

"We ran into each other about a week later, and we've been together ever since." Rafe rubbed my shoulders. "I like to think I've changed for the better from knowing Peter."

My face warmed. "Don't lay it on too thick."

He smiled. "He embarrasses easily."

Stephany gave me a sympathetic glance. "Can't really blame him. I mean, we're all staring at him like he's an animal in the zoo."

"I understand you're curious. My mom grilled Rafe plenty when she first met him."

"Did she?" Mrs. Hexton clapped her hands. "Good."

"Good?" Rafe laughed. "Why good?"

"Well because that shows she cares. If she had no interest in her son's alpha, that would be sad." Mrs. Hexton leaned forward. "What about your father, Peter?"

I dropped my gaze. "I'm afraid he died when I was eighteen."

"Awww." Stephany pushed her lip out. "That's terrible."

"It was awful." I agreed. "I hope to be as good a dad as mine was."

"My guess is you will be," Tom said quietly. "Anybody can be instructed on how to change a diaper, or give a baby a bottle. But to be a good dad you have to care, and you obviously do care, Peter. That's the part you can't be taught."

My heart squeezed tight at his kind words. "I hope so. I've wanted to have a baby since I was old enough to know omegas could have babies." I laughed stiffly. "It was just something I've always wanted."

"Me too." Mrs. Hexton met my gaze, nodding. "And it's nothing to be ashamed of. If an omega doesn't want to have a baby, I'm all for their right not to. But that doesn't negate our right to want to have a child either. Live and let live, that's my motto."

"Yeah," I said softly. "I agree. It's a personal decision."

Rafe cleared his throat. "So now let's talk about what an amazing alpha I am." He puffed out his chest.

I grinned. "I think you do that enough already without us jumping in."

He laughed. "Ouch."

I put my head on his shoulder and smiled up at him. "All kidding aside, you're everything I ever wanted in an alpha."

He nodded, amusement dancing in his eyes. "I thought I probably was."

****

As the pregnancy progressed, so did my physical discomfort. By eight and a half months, my back ached anytime I stood for long periods of time, and constipation was just the status quo.

I let Rafe talk me into a day on the boat one sunny Saturday morning. I gave in to his cajoling because I felt like such a stick in the mud most of the time, and I didn't want him to get bored with me.

To be honest, the last thing in the world I wanted was to be on a boat in the ocean. But considering I felt like a bloated whale, I guess it was the most fitting place for me. We didn't leave the harbor because that way there was less chance of me getting sea sick.

"Do you want more prune juice?" Rafe asked, without even opening his eyes. He was reclined on a lounge chair next to me, and he looked so content I was jealous.

I cringed and glanced at the champagne flute half full of the hideous juice. "God no."

He chuckled. "It's good for your... er... problem."

"No thanks. Just because you put it in a pretty glass, it's still disgusting."

"It's not *that* bad."

I squinted at him. "How would you know? When is the last time you drank prune juice?"

He shuddered. "Oh, god. I never drink that crap. It's gross."

I laughed unwillingly. "You're such a jerk."

He grinned and his dimples were deep in his tanned cheeks. "I know."

I rested my head against the back of my chair, shifting my hips and trying to find a comfortable position. Of course, there weren't any. "Just two more weeks and this part will be over," I grumbled.

He lifted his head to look at me. "I'm terrified of when the kid is really here. Are you?"

"No. I can't wait."

He frowned. "But it's so compact this way. Once it's here, we'll have to drag a diaper bag and playpen everywhere we go. This way the baby is just self-contained."

"Has it escaped your notice I'm miserable?" I chuffed.

"No." He laughed. "You won't let me forget."

I scowled. "Oh, I see… you want me to suffer in silence?"

"Would that be okay?" He gave me a cocky grin. "You really do whine a lot."

"Oh, my god!" I grabbed the folded towel near me and launched it at his head.

He caught it mid-air, laughing. "What? What did I say wrong?"

I snorted a laugh, but when a painful twinge jabbed me in the gut, I sucked in a big breath. I pressed my hand to my stomach. "Ouch."

He frowned. "You okay?"

"I think so. I just had a pain, that's all."

He studied me in silence. "Let me know if you have another—"

"Ow!" I winced. "That feels really weird."

He stood and came to me, kneeling down, his expression serious. "Have you had any other pains lately, or spotting?"

"None."

"Okay. Good." He sighed. "It's not that unusual to have a few contractions as you near your due date."

I rubbed my tummy. "I've had some weird sensations the last week like my stomach is tightening. It's hard to describe."

"But no bloody discharge or actual pain?"

"No. Nothing like that."

He nodded. "I think that's normal."

He sat back down and, just as he picked up his champagne glass, another jab hit me.

I winced. "Damn, that pain is back."

He studied me warily. "Would you say it's actually pain or discomfort?"

"Pain."

"Hmmm."

Another stab spiked through me. "Shit. I don't remember feeling anything like this before. This is definitely different."

He stood and rubbed his jaw. "You're eight and a half weeks. You do realize the baby could arrive any day now, right?"

I swallowed and nodded. "In theory." I tried not to think about it too much. While I wanted a baby, I was of course nervous about the actual delivery.

I pressed my stomach, feeling discomfort around my bladder. "I think maybe I need to pee."

He held out his hand. "Come on. I'll help you." He pulled me to my feet, and just as I was fully upright, a flush of warm fluid went down my inner thighs. I widened my eyes. "Shit. Wha... what does that mean?" I knew what it meant, or at least, I had a terrifying guess.

"Oh, boy." His voice wobbled. "I think you're in labor."

"But... but..." I glanced around at the water and the boats. "I can't be in labor."

He wasn't listening. He put his arm around my waist. "Come with me." He led me toward the cabins. "Let's get you on a bed. I don't want this kid coming out and hitting its head on the damn deck."

"No. No. This can't really be happening." I sounded as panicked as I felt.

He got me down the stairs and to the guest bedroom, then he had me sit on the edge of the queen sized bed. "I'm going to go tell the captain to head in immediately." When I groaned and fell back on the bed writhing in pain, he shook his head. "Shit. I think I'm going to have to deliver the baby, Peter."

I bugged my eyes. "You? You can't deliver our baby."

"Of course I can, if I have to."

"No. That's nuts."

"I haven't done it in about five years, but you do realize I went to medical school, right?" He moved to the door. "I'll be right back. Stay in bed." He left the room, banging the door behind him.

Another jolt hit me, and I groaned, clutching my stomach. The pains were coming faster now, and there was an uncomfortable pressure on my rectum. I moaned and squirmed in pain, waiting for Rafe to return. This was unbelievable. I couldn't grasp that the one time I was nowhere near the hospital, I was about to give birth. I felt terrified and lost, especially without Rafe by my side.

After about ten minutes, Rafe returned with a stack of towels and a pot of hot water. He slipped on gloves, and he examined the area between my legs. "Yeah, this kid is definitely coming."

"Shit, really?" I squeaked, grimacing with pain.

"Now, Peter, you need to listen to me." He gave me a stern look. "I need you to push only when I say so. You're going to want to push all the time, but we need to do this in the right way."

I nodded, sweat running down my forehead. "I'll try."

He grabbed my legs and pulled me to the end of the bed. I kicked off my shoes, and he tugged my jeans and briefs off and tossed them on the floor. "Bend your knees." His voice was emotionless.

"Are you sure you can do this?" I gasped, as another contraction slammed into me.

He nodded. "Yes."

"But you just see patients at your office." I panted.

"Peter, I'm a board certified RE."

"I don't know what that means," I groaned, rolling my hips around.

"It means…" His voice was patient. "I went an extra five years to complete ten years of post-graduate training. I'm certified as both and

OB/GYN and also a reproductive endocrinology and infertility specialist. It means I can deliver this baby with my eyes closed."

I nodded, holding his bright gaze. "Okay." I swallowed. "And… and most importantly you're my alpha." I needed to say that. I could see he'd kicked into doctor mode, which was awesome, but I also needed the support of my alpha right now.

His gaze softened. "Yes. I'm right here. I won't let anything bad happen to you or our baby."

"Okay," I wheezed, convulsing my muscles as a spasm hit. I dug my heels into the mattress and cried out. It felt like my body was being ripped in two, and I shivered against the pain. I'd assumed I'd give birth in the hospital. I'd planned on an epidural, but now I was here, stuck on a damn boat, about to pop my baby out with zero pain medication. I felt like crying. I'd never been one of those omegas who thought I wanted a natural childbirth. Hell no. I'd been a hundred percent planning on using the wonders of modern science to get me through.

He pulled up a chair and perched between my thighs. "Okay, you're doing great." His voice was calm, and he kept his eyes trained on the area where the baby would appear. "I need you to give a little push when the next contraction hits. Okay? We'll let mother nature help us out a little."

"All right." I was already tired from the pain, but I knew there was much more needed from me.

It wasn't long before another contraction rolled through me. I clenched my teeth and pushed as he'd instructed, letting out a yell.

"Good. Good. Okay now stop. *Stop*." His voice was urgent. "Back off, Peter. Relax your muscles."

I wanted to keep pushing desperately, but I listened to his voice. My lower half was almost numb from the pain, and I felt slightly nauseated. "Why can't I push?" I whined.

"You don't want to hurt the baby or tear, right?"

"Yeah," I moaned. "Okay." The urge to push was almost overwhelming, but I clung to the sound of his steady voice.

"Next contraction we're doing the same thing. You're doing great, Peter. Really great."

I nodded and bit my lower lip as a tear trickled out of the corner of my eye. I was in agony and I felt like passing out, but I just focused on Rafe's husky voice, and the warm golden brown of his eyes. Another contraction rolled around. "Oh, shit."

"Okay, Peter, here we go again. Just like last time, push when I tell you to, and then stop."

"I'll try."

I had no idea how much time passed as we continued that pattern of me pushing, and him talking to me quietly. Every inch of my body ached, and there were moments when my yells of agony almost drowned out his voice. But he just kept talking and reassuring me through it all. At the end of each contraction, he was there, his smile warm and his voice steady. In that moment I truly trusted him. The only thing that kept me from losing control was the sound of his deep voice guiding me, encouraging me. He was my alpha, and I knew he'd protect me and our baby at all cost.

The pain was so intense, I almost lost consciousness a few times. I was sweaty, and the smell of blood filled my nostrils. Rafe's movements were slow and methodical as he grabbed towels and told me what to do. Eventually, after what felt like hours and hours, there was a gurgling squeal from the baby, and the relief on Rafe's face forced a sob from my throat. That was the first glimpse I'd got that he'd been scared too. Maybe even terrified of a bad outcome.

His expression, as he held our child, just made my tears slip out of my eyes faster. I think up until that very second, I'd secretly been afraid he'd reject our baby. I'd harbored the fear that maybe he'd only told me what I'd wanted to hear. But the look of wonder on his features was all I needed to see to be reassured that he was a hundred percent in this with me and our child.

He sniffed, and moved to clean off the infant, and snip the umbilical cord. Then he put the crying child on my chest. His eyes were red rimmed as he set the baby down. "It's a boy." His voice was hushed.

"Really?" I kissed the wiggling baby's head, feeling joyful. The memory of the pain of labor was just that; a memory. The baby was here. The baby was safe.

"Yeah." He sniffed some more, as if trying to hold back his emotions. "You did it, Peter."

"We did it," I whispered, touching the chubby cheek of the infant. "I was so scared."

He clenched his jaw and nodded.

I kissed the baby again, feeling in awe of the little thing. "You have horrible timing, kid." I put my arms around the baby and, even though he wiggled and whimpered, I smiled. "I can't believe I'm holding my baby."

Rafe wiped at his eyes. "Yeah. You finally have your baby." He sat beside me on the bed, and he wiped again impatiently at his eyes. "Shit, my eyes keep dripping."

"Nothing wrong with that. You're allowed to be emotional."

"I guess." He sighed and stroked my hair off my brow. "I'm thankful you didn't hemorrhage."

I gulped. "Shit. Me too."

He touched the baby's soft fuzzy head. "We're also lucky there were no complications with the birth or the baby. I don't know that I could have handled anything too challenging on my own out here on a yacht."

I frowned at his blunt statement. "Wow. You hid all those fears really well. I just thought you were in control of the situation."

He smiled at me, a worry line between his eyes. "I was as in control as I could be under the circumstances."

There was a knock on the bedroom door, and a deckhand poked his head in. "Sorry to bother you, Dr. Hexton, but Captain Phillips said we'll be docking in five minutes."

"Thank you, Carl," Rafe responded.

"I should clean up." I didn't want to let go of my son, but I knew I was a bloody mess. We both needed to be checked out at the hospital, and I couldn't walk off the boat like this. "Is it okay if I stand up?"

"Yeah. Just move slowly."

"Okay." The baby was fussy, and I assumed he was hungry, but I didn't know the first thing about breast feeding. I'd read a few books on lactation the last month, but to be honest, the very idea of it kind of freaked me out.

Rafe lifted the baby, and my heart melted when he kissed the child. He tenderly swaddled the infant in a towel, as I moved slowly to sit up. My body throbbed, obviously sore from the trauma of giving birth. I stood hesitantly, noting some bloody towels strewn over the carpet and the mattress.

It looks like a war zone.

Eying the blood covering my legs, he said, "If you think you're up to it, you can rinse off in the shower. Don't use soap near your rectum. They'll handle any chance of infection at the hospital. There's a seat in the shower, I recommend you sit, so you don't faint." He frowned. "I'd help you but I can't leave the baby."

"I'm fine. Don't worry about it." I walked gingerly toward the bathroom, biting my lip against the pain. Once inside the small bathroom, I sat on the toilet, waiting until the dizziness passed. Then I slowly moved to turn on the shower water. I stepped carefully into the cubicle, and soaped my upper body and legs, avoiding the area where the baby had come out. The shower had a hand held spray head, so I gently doused that tender spot with clean warm water and nothing else.

Once I was done, I dried off and wrapped the towel around my waist. When I came out of the bathroom, Rafe had some clothes ready for me. I changed, and Rafe handed me the sleeping infant.

"Is it normal for him to be so sleepy?" I asked, studying the babies pink cheeks.

"Yeah. He's been through a trauma just like you." He grimaced. "Be glad he's asleep because when he wakes up he'll be hungry."

I gritted my teeth. "God. I'll have to figure out how to nurse him."

"The nurses will help you at the hospital." He put his arm around me and glanced down at our sleeping son. "I can't believe he's here."

I smiled. "I know."

"He's so damn cute." Rafe squinted. "I just want to protect him from anything in life that could ever hurt him."

"Me too."

He kissed the side of my head. "I feel weirdly content."

"I think that sensation is called happiness."

"The funny thing is… I thought I was happy."

I searched his face. "Maybe you were."

He shook his head. "Not really."

"But now you are?"

"I'm embarrassingly happy."

I rested my head on his shoulder with a contented sigh. "Me too."

Epilogue

"I don't think he likes me." Stewart gave me a worried look as the crying baby wiggled in his arms. "Shhh, Luke. It's okay."

I laughed. "He can probably sense you're afraid of him."

"I'm not afraid. I just don't know what to do with him."

"Talk to him," Rafe urged. "He likes that."

Stewart glanced down at the baby. "Hey, kid. I'm your Uncle Stewart." When the baby spit up, all three of us groaned.

I jumped forward and took the baby from my friend. "That means he likes you." I grimaced, meeting Rafe's amused gaze.

Stewart dabbed at his shirt with the burp cloth I'd handed him. "I seem to affect a lot of people this way."

I laughed. "Stop." I sat on the sofa.

Sighing, Stewart smiled. "I'd offer to babysit, but I don't think Luke or I would enjoy that."

"Don't worry. Peter refuses to leave the baby with anyone yet anyhow." Rafe gave me an affectionate glance. "He's being a protective daddy."

I stroked Luke's chubby cheek. "You just hear so many horror stories."

"I know." Rafe nodded.

Stewart cleared his throat. "Not to change the subject, but I wondered if I could get some advice from you guys."

"What kind of advice?" I asked.

"Romantic."

"Not sure I'll be much good." Rafe looked non-plussed.

"If you don't mind, I'd kind of love to get your perspective... you know... as an alpha." Stewart studied Rafe.

I was surprised he'd want Rafe's advice. He hadn't seemed that thrilled with my alpha in the beginning. Although, I had to admit, he'd warmed up to him, now that Rafe had shown he was really in this relationship with me.

"I guess. If you really want my opinion." Rafe laughed uneasily.

"Is there a particular guy you're interested in?" I squinted at my friend. He hadn't really told me about anyone he'd been dating.

He bit his lip, his cheeks flushed. "That guy Lex is back in town."

"Lex? Oh, you mean that alpha who stood up for you when that asshole from Grindr mistook you for someone else?"

"Yeah."

I fixed my curious gaze on my friend. "I wondered what ever happened with that. It's been a while."

Stewart shrugged. "I thought he was interested in me, but then he had to leave the area for a job."

I frowned. "Really?"

"Yeah. He took a job on a ranch for a friend of his in Australia."

"He couldn't get work right here?" Rafe frowned.

Wincing, Stewart said, "I got the feeling this friend was more than just a Platonic buddy. Lex was conflicted about going, but he did end up leaving." Stewart looked confused. "I don't know what that means, or why he'd want to get together with me now that he's back. It's been over eight months."

"Maybe that friend in Australia really was just a friend." I patted Luke's back as I spoke.

"Maybe." Stewart didn't seem convinced.

"Did you have sex with this Lex guy?" Rafe asked bluntly.

Stewart's face turned red. "Once."

"Oh. Well, that does change things." I frowned. "Do you really like him?"

"Yeah, but I don't want to get hurt." He shifted his gaze to Rafe. "I don't want to just be a booty call when he's in town. I want something more."

"You should probably make that clear to him," Rafe said, glancing at me. "Alphas aren't mind readers. If you sleep with us, and we've made it clear we don't want more, we figure you know the score."

Nodding, Stewart said, "I know. But it's awkward to have that conversation since we've only been with each other once."

"Well, he called you. That's a good sign." I spoke brightly. I'd only met Lex that one time, and he'd seemed like a good guy. "He didn't strike me as a player. You should get together with him and pump him for info on this mystery friend in Australia. Then you'd know whether he's worth your time or not."

Stewart hung his head. "I wish I didn't like him so much. It would make ignoring him easier."

Rafe laughed. "God, that's exactly what I used to say about Peter."

I grinned. "But ultimately, he couldn't resist me."

"That's the truth." Rafe sighed.

Stewart watched us. "I want what you two have. I want someone completely into me and only me." He gave a stiff laugh. "God, I didn't want that at all just a year ago. In fact, if a guy seemed really interested, I'd bail."

"You're maturing. Sometimes the baby bug hits later in life."

"I'll tell you one thing..." Rafe's voice was firm. "When an alpha wants you, he goes after you. Period."

"Okay," Stewart said softly.

"Is Lex looking to settle down?" I asked.

"I don't know. Like I said, we only had one night together." He swallowed. "It was a fucking good night too. Then we made plans to meet up the next day, but he called and told me he was leaving the country." Grimacing, Stewart raked a hand through his hair. "It hurt my feelings to be honest."

"Did he try to talk to you when he was away?" Rafe asked.

"I got one drunken text." He bit his lip.

"What did it say?" I perked up.

He sighed. "That he wished he wasn't such a fucking coward."

"What does that mean?" I turned to look at Rafe.

Wrinkling his brow, Rafe said, "I'm not sure. Sounds to me like he wishes he'd stayed here and pursued things with you maybe. But I'm just guessing."

"Yeah." Stewart stood. "Thanks for the advice."

"Of course." Rafe nodded.

"Did you agree to meet him?" I asked.

"I haven't decided." Stewart shifted uneasily. "Like I said, I don't want to get hurt. Lex is the kind of guy that could wiggle in and do damage."

"Understood." I gave my friend a sympathetic look.

"I'll let you two know what happens." He waved and left the house.

Once he'd gone, Rafe sat beside me on the couch. "I'm so glad I don't have to worry about all that stuff anymore."

"Me too." I sometimes couldn't believe my luck in finding Rafe. We'd had such a rocky start, that to finally be settled and in love was a miracle.

Rafe put his arm around me. "My little family is all I need."

I smiled at him and then down at our son. We truly were a family. Having it all had seemed like an impossible dream not that long ago. But then I'd met Rafe, and I'd taken a chance, and even sleepless nights, and dirty diapers couldn't wipe the big grin off my face.

OTHER BOOKS BY BEAU BROWN

Omega Lover Book #1

Omega Daddy Book #2

Omega's Choice Book #3

Omega Lover Box Set

The Sherriff Surrenders #1

(Book One Written by my pal E.E. Wilde)

The Manny Tames the Cowboy #2

Stealing A Cowboy's Heart #3

Copyright (c) 2018 by Beau Brown

Baby Doctor

All rights reserved

No part of this book may be reproduced or
transmitted in any form or by any means,
electronic or mechanical, including photocopying,
recording, or by any information storage and
retrieval system, without written permission from
Beau Brown at beaubrown333@mail.com

This is a work of fiction. Any resemblance to
persons living or dead is entirely coincidental.

***

*CLICK HERE TO JOIN MY MAILING
LIST!*